DREW HAMILTON

BOULDER Boys:

MAX AND SAM

Boulder Boys: Max and Sam
©2015 Drew Hamilton

Licensed material is being used for illustrative purposes only and any person depicted in the licensed material is a model.
Cover art and formatting by Reese Dante www.reesedante.com
Edited by Pam Ebeler and Kris Esgar

Edition/ISBN
Paperback: 978-0-9973436-0-1
Kindle: 978-0-9973436-1-8
Epub: 978-0-9973436-2-5

First Edition October, 2015
Printed in the United States of America

This work is M/M fiction with language and situations appropriate for adults only. All characters engaged in romantic activities are over the age of eighteen.

Dedication

To my Grandmother, who first ignited the spark to write.

1

April 1997

The scenario always started out the same, we rarely deviated from our established routine. It would usually start after we completed our workout. I have no idea why he liked to instigate things between us when we were hot and sweaty, but it was his way.

He had a couple signals to indicate impending mischief; a quirked brow or a slow smile. He always had a look that promised a good time. He liked to strip buck naked and let his hard body do the talking.

I liked the fact that we weren't evenly matched, he being a good four or five-inches shorter. I've always been attracted to guys shorter and smaller than me. As far as our dicks were concerned, we were pretty even; we had the same length, but mine was a little thicker. We generally spent a minute or two comparing boners, making none of our critical measurements had changed.

He would step closer, toe-to-toe, and press the tip of his cock to my pubic bone. If feeling especially energetic, he would stand on top of my feet and tease that he was a couple of inches taller.

What a joker.

He would put his hand on my hips and rub his hard dick against mine. It always felt so amazing. There wasn't much talking, other than an urgent request to rub harder or faster. Sometimes he would reach down and play with my balls. It was always special when he did that.

I remember wanting to kiss him desperately, but I always woke up before we got to that stage of the game.

I was having some seriously naughty dreams. They started at the beginning of my freshman year in college and were still going strong. The weirdest part of all, I had no idea who the guy was. I'd never seen him in my life and never seemed to get to the point in the dream where we exchanged names.

I was having a good time with my freshman year at the University of Colorado. I had graduated in the class of 1996 at Boulder High School, so the transition wasn't a big one. So far, the main differences were harder classes, a lot more freedom, and better food options at lunch. I still lived at home with my parents and my little brother Morgan.

Morgan wasn't that little. He's fourteen months younger and planned to join me at CU next fall. He had an outstanding year playing varsity quarterback.

Morgan and I are practically carbon copies, both six-foot tall, muscular, and good-looking. When people met us for the first time, they would invariably ask if we were twins. Even though we looked alike, we had a few differences. I played baseball in high school, and he was better with math and science. We've always been good students in our other classes, with history being his notable exception. Morgan tended to be a little more carefree, while I was more cautious. When he got out of line, I was the one invariably tasked to bring him back to Earth. I liked to call him "Squirt", to get his attention and keep him from doing something stupid.

Morgan and I had always been best friends because we were so close in age and because we grew up as army brats who had to move around all the time. Our parents met while serving in the Army at the Landstuhl Regional Medical Center in Germany. Mom was a psychiatrist and Dad was a medic. Since Mom was an officer and Dad was enlisted, they had to wait until Mom's term of service was up to marry. I came along eight months later; guess they couldn't wait that extra month.

The dream left me with a dilemma, because it was a wet one. I needed to clean up, but there was a problem—Morgan and I shared a bedroom. We were in the basement with an attached bath, so I didn't have to worry about waking Mom and Dad, but I didn't need added scrutiny from my inquisitive brother. He was like our parents, if he caught wind of something, he could be tenacious until he got a satisfactory answer.

I got out of bed as gently as possible. I was cautious because sometimes Morgan was a heavy sleeper and other times, not so much. Sometimes, I had to throw a pillow or shake the hell out of him to get him to wake up and other times, he would jolt out of bed at the slightest noise. I tiptoed to the bathroom with a plan, I could deal with damp boxers as long as I cleaned up the inside with a washcloth. A clean pair was out of the question because the dresser was at the head of Morgan's bed.

I congratulated myself for my cleverness, I flushed the toilet to mask the sound of running water from the sink. I wasn't going to take the time to worry about using hot water, I went for cleanliness over comfort.

I went into my stealthy Ninja mode and shut off the bathroom light before I opened the door. I was relieved to put this situation behind me for another day. I knew I would need to act on my impulses at some point and college seemed a good place to do it, but the fact I lived at home and not in the dorms was problematic. My situation was typical of gay guys my age, I was too young to go to the bars, plus Dad kept Morgan and me on a tight leash.

I discovered a new problem when I opened the door, Morgan was standing there with a grin. "Must have been a good one, huh?"

I began to think about the wonderful possibility of a long camping trip by myself before answering him. "Go back to bed, Squirt."

Instead of going to his bed, he took a seat on mine. Now that the cat was out of the bag, I could change out of my damp underwear. I knew better than to expect any privacy from him. As he made sure I put my fresh underwear on correctly, he asked, "Would you like to talk about it?"

"No," I shrugged out of my boxers and quickly put on a fresh pair. I glanced over to my bed, Morgan was stretched out with his hands behind his head. We were going to talk whether I wanted to or not.

"Max, you've been having these dreams a lot." There was a significant pause before he continued. "I thought we agreed not to hide things from each other."

Damn he was observant. "How would you know how many dreams I've been having?"

He grinned, "You're a moaner..."

Lovely.

I didn't know what to say, all I knew was I didn't want to talk about it. It felt weird having those discussions with him. Much of it had to do with the fact that we're both gay. Morgan was the first one to admit it when he was thirteen. I confessed the same to him a few months later. It made me uncomfortable to discuss anything sex-related with Morgan because he was kind of hot; I was afraid of crossing a line that couldn't be uncrossed. We used to jerk-off together when we were younger, but I put a stop to it when he turned fifteen. It was too strange and intense. That was probably why I was having dreams in the first place because our close proximity didn't lead to a lot of private time.

Morgan didn't share the same problem when it came to talking about those things. "I find it hard to believe you haven't found some hottie at CU." He sized me up for a few moments and I started to feel uncomfortable. "We could start jerking-off again..." He held up his hand when I started to object. "Max, we need to get past this...you're hot and I am too, so fucking what? We can masturbate in the same room and behave. It will take away some of the pressure until we each meet someone."

I yawned dramatically. "Let's talk about this in the morning, it's late and I need my sleep. Tomorrow is a running day."

Morgan rolled his eyes and pointed at the clock. "We might as well stay up, it's four-thirty."

I hadn't paid any attention to the time. Morgan was right, we got up at four-forty-five because Dad liked to start our Physical Training session at five am sharp. I got up from the tiny section of the bed that wasn't taken up by Morgan, and went to the basement refrigerator for a bottle of water. "You're right, as usual."

"Bring me one back too."

Morgan was still sprawled out on my bed when I returned. I had a feeling the interrogation was far from over. I stood there for a moment and watched him. He looked up at me. "What?"

"Just ask me what you want to know and get it over with."

"Max, I'm not that bad."

I sat beside him. "You're worse than Mom and Dad put together." I decided to crack a joke. "If you ever decide to go into something besides computer programming, you would make an excellent lawyer."

Morgan ignored my snark. "You haven't told me anything about the guy in your dream. Is he someone you know?"

I shook my head. "Don't worry, it's not Embry Salazar. I know how much you like him."

Morgan took a long drink of water. "He's fucking hot."

"Morgan, he's a total dick."

My brother smiled at me. "He's just that way with you because you're not into football."

"I think playing on the varsity baseball team for four years was a pretty good accomplishment, along with my full-ride scholarship, courtesy of the United States Army."

Morgan smiled broader. "He's going to CU in the fall with me, but he's not playing football, maybe he'll be nicer to you."

"I'll believe it when I see it."

Morgan looked up at me again. "You're deflecting, what does the guy of your dreams look like?"

"His hair is dark brown and he's super cute. He has a very nice body."

Morgan zeroed in for the ultimate question. "How tall is he?"

"I didn't have a tape measure in the dream."

"Come on," he pleaded. "Just answer me."

"Maybe five-foot-seven? I'm not sure, he's a little shorter than me."

Morgan shook his head. "I don't understand why you get such a charge out of the little guys."

"Aren't you supposed to ask what his dick is like?" I shook my head, "I'm not sure you're really gay."

Morgan laughed at me. "You want someone little so you can carry them around, don't you?"

"Squirt, I can easily carry someone bigger and you know that." Our dad had us heft each other around in a fireman's carry all the time. He felt it was a good muscle and character builder. He was doing his best to keep me prepared for life in the Army. Mom made it clear she would only support me joining the military if I did so as an officer. Deep down, my dad wanted me to follow in his footsteps as a medic and then a drill sergeant. I wasn't quite sure what I wanted to do yet. My main concern was passing college and the ROTC qualification course in-between my junior and senior year. I still had time to make up my mind about what I wanted to do in the service and my grades were good enough to open up a lot of opportunities if I wanted to do something different.

The thought of being in Special Forces was particularly interesting. If I mentioned it to my dad, he would get a proud gleam in his eye. Mom didn't share the same sentiment, she usually stormed out of the room if I brought it up.

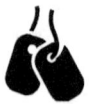

It was beautiful spring morning when Morgan and I met Dad for our morning run. We followed the same PT routine Dad used with trainees, working out six days a week. Three of those days were taken up with a three-mile sprint. The other three were a combination of muscle exercises: push-ups, sit-ups, and calisthenics, followed by a shorter one-mile jog. When the weather was bad, we had two treadmills and a weight bench in the basement.

Morgan and I shared a bedroom because the other basement bedroom was our workout room. Neither of us wanted to sleep upstairs in our parents' domain, so we dealt with sleeping in the same room. It wasn't really that bad, I slept better with him close by. Not that I ever told him that.

I'd been thinking about being in the Army a lot. It was weird, but the guy in my dream had a military vibe about him. It seemed natural to me that since the service had been good to my parents, it would be good to me as well. Uncle Sam paid for my mom's education so she could be a doctor and my parents met while serving their country. I was hoping for something along the same lines. *Don't Ask, Don't Tell* didn't seem that big of an obstacle, because being gay was not the first thing that entered peoples mind when they met me.

Dad enjoyed his time as a medic, but eventually wanted to do something different. When he was accepted to drill sergeant school, we moved from Germany to Fort Jackson, South Carolina. Once he finished with his extensive training, we were off to Fort Dix, New Jersey. Over the years, we moved every two or three years to other posts as Dad's career progressed. We lived in Missouri at Fort Leonard Wood, Fort Knox in Kentucky, Fort Sill in Oklahoma, and finally back to Fort Jackson, where Dad served the remainder of his enlistment and retired. Mom always found a job treating patients wherever we moved. Since she was psychiatrist, she was also a fully qualified MD. Sometimes she worked in general practice if there wasn't a psychiatry job available. She loved doing both.

Out of all the places Dad had been assigned, South Carolina was our favorite. We did a lot of traveling when Mom and Dad had time off, the beach was an hour away in one direction and the mountains were about the same in the other. Washington, DC was a day's drive and Atlanta and Savannah were even closer. Morgan and I learned how to play golf in South Carolina, even though we weren't that good. We became serious athletes during our time in Oklahoma, where we both started playing baseball. Morgan switched to football in South

Carolina. Dad was always happy to make sure we were in top shape so we could excel at our chosen sports.

When Dad retired, my folks decided to return to Boulder, where they both grew up. Dad's parents had passed away, months apart, while we were in Oklahoma and left him a sprawling fifties-era ranch house that was fully paid for. It also had a huge barn in the back yard where my grandpa, and now Dad, kept all his woodworking tools. My grandparents on my mother's side moved to Arizona after she joined the Army.

Boulder had been a pleasant surprise for Morgan and me. We expected to freeze our asses off all winter because we were used to warmer climates. We weren't prepared for over three-hundred sunny days a year and temperatures that frequently reached the seventies during the day—in the middle of winter. Too bad we weren't better at golf, the courses were open year-round.

While the winters weren't too bad, summers in Colorado were truly something to behold. The lack of humidity and bugs were a welcome difference from the Deep South. Running in such a high-altitude took some getting used to, but we adapted. The temperature rarely got above the upper-eighties and the evenings were cool and comfortable. The sheer number of things we could do outdoors was almost overwhelming. There were hiking and bike trails everywhere, and we took advantage of them frequently. One of our favorite pastimes was people watching at the outdoor Pearl Street Mall.

The only thing anyone ever gave Morgan and me trouble about were our accents, courtesy of our time in South Carolina and Kentucky. It didn't bother us because it made us stand out. The fact that we did such a good job with our athletics helped cement our popularity. The only possible drawback I could think of was Morgan and I didn't have many close friends. Our responsibilities to our academics, sports, and helping our dad, didn't leave us much time for hanging out with others after school or going to parties.

At any rate, it was much more convenient to live with my best friend. I knew Morgan felt the same way, but we didn't really talk about it.

When Dad retired, he took up woodworking full-time to keep himself busy, make extra money, and teach us a trade in the event we ever needed it. He learned from his dad and wanted to continue the family tradition. Dad's specialty was kitchen cabinets and furniture. He had enough orders to keep the three of us busy and was looking to hire someone to help out.

During the school year, we helped as much as we could, mainly on the weekends. Once summer came around, we were expected to help in the shop daily, until four in the afternoon. He taught us responsibility and paid us for our time. We made more than most guys our age who worked retail or fast-food.

On our way back to the house from our run, Morgan motioned to a house down the street from ours. There was a real estate sign in the front yard with a sold sign bolted to the top. "Maybe someone cool will be moving in."

It would have been amazing if it was the guy I'd been dreaming about, but I didn't give it much more thought because we had a busy day ahead of us.

2

May 1997

My dreams continued unabated. In fact, they became much more intense. I still had no idea what his name was. The dreams were starting to get longer, in one of them I noticed his sexy southern accent when he told me to kiss him. He had expressive brown eyes with impossibly long lashes. His lean body, with its impressive definition was intoxicating. Sometimes I carried him around, and that was a completely new level of hot I never considered before. One thing was for sure, he would give Morgan's lust interest, Embry Salazar, a run for his money and he wasn't a dick.

I did *everything* with this yet to-be-named guy in my dreams. When I mention everything, I'm talking about what obviously comes to mind, but it went way beyond the pedestrian or the usual. The dreams were almost like a movie sequence where we went everywhere together. We were a couple in the dreams and I really liked the thought of that. We went shopping and hiking together. We had lunch and dinner together. We also worked side-by-side in Dad's shop. Dad seemed to take a special interest in him and it made the possibility of coming out to him and Mom much less scary.

As the dreams progressed, our surroundings started to become clearer. I could tell we were having sex in a place that wasn't a normal bedroom, once I concentrated and tried to remember. As I thought more about the dreams in my waking hours, I realized I was with the mystery guy in surroundings best described as opulent. The dreams began to slowly morph to where I could see more of what was around us. In the beginning, they were sort of hazy. We were having awesome sexual encounters in a house straight out of the gilded age. As the days went on, there was almost a constant niggling at the back of my mind about it. Why would I fantasize about sex with another guy in a setting out of *Lifestyles of the Rich and Famous*? Fortunately, I didn't have the time to dwell on it because Dad's business was really taking off. He had orders for ten sets of kitchen cabinets that would take us all summer to complete. Dad placed an ad in *Westword*, looking for someone who could help us.

At least I had the smarts to keep a hand towel tucked under my bed when my dreams became really hot.

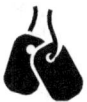

Morgan and I were so busy helping our dad, most of the time we stayed in the shop until five or six in the evening. Dad could tell it was starting to wear on us, and one day told us to take the rest of the day off when we broke for lunch. He wanted us to take the Jeep out for a spin and have some fun for a change. Our shared 1975 Jeep Cherokee was the perfect vehicle for Colorado and us; built like a tank with four-wheel drive. The body was grey with a white top.

Morgan and I did a good job saving our money because we had little time to spend any of it. We decided to part with some of it at McDonalds for Big Macs, extra-large fries and Cokes. We won the french fry lottery that day, ours were fresh from the fryer. Our lunch was so good; we barely spoke while eating.

I didn't have a clue what I wanted to do. Pearl Street Mall was kind of fun, but a person could only look at tie-dye t-shirts, incense and hemp products so much. We got plenty of exercise, so I didn't want to go on a major hike. Dad preferred to go with us when hiking in the foothills because of the wildlife. We knew to listen to what our parents told us. If we ended up in emergency room and Mom found out, we would be grounded until we were forty.

I smiled at my brother when he turned up the french fry carton and poured the last tiny bits into his mouth. I was surprised he didn't lick the paper liner to get every last grain of salt. "Any idea what you want to do?"

Morgan, the event planner, nodded enthusiastically. "I want to go check out that old house."

I shook my head with fervor. I had a lot of practice when it came to Morgan and his ridiculous ideas.

"Come on, don't be such a pussy."

Last summer, Morgan and I discovered a huge old mansion on one of our drives into the foothills. Since we were young and stupid, we looked first and did our research later. It was a big mansion, which we learned was neoclassical style. It was also the site of a grisly murder-suicide in 1964. Two best friends from Boulder, Jason Buchanan and Rick Andrews were alone in the house one Saturday evening after Jason's parents went to a party in Denver. No one knew for sure what happened, except that Jason was shot in the stomach and his best friend took a bullet in the head. A horrific fire gutted the mansion moments after the shooting. At least that's what the investigators believed.

Locals in the area were certain the mansion and the associated grounds were haunted. The site was rumored to be a sacred Indian burial ground because many artifacts were found in the surrounding area. Kids from our high school told thrilling stories about driving out to the house and being assaulted by screaming voices and pelted by stones and tree branches. As a result, nobody went anywhere near the place.

My brother was a sucker for stories like that. He loved looking at anything abandoned or with an interesting history. We had been there a couple of times before and nothing happened. On the far edge of the property was a huge pond with a smooth pebbled bottom and a dock. We went skinny-dipping the last time we were there.

Morgan begged me to go in the house with him both times. Having strict parents caused me to think like them from time-to-time. I could imagine falling through the floor into the basement or having part of the roof cave in on us. Needless to say, I wasn't very excited about the idea. I searched for every tool in my arsenal to get him to change his mind. Threats weren't very good because I couldn't come up with any. It was ridiculous for me to bribe him because he had tons of cash already. There was one thing he would agree to, but I didn't want to go there.

Morgan got a big smile and leaned in to whisper. "I promise I won't bug you to go in the house. Fear not, I won't try to get you to jerk off with me either."

Damn, he could totally read my mind. "Do you swear?"

He nodded. "I won't put you in danger Maxwell, I swear."

His response had a certain lawyerly vagueness to it that gave me pause. It was probably stupid, but I agreed.

Once we were in the Jeep, Morgan turned and asked, "You will go swimming with me, right?"

"Yes, Squirt, we can go swimming. That's probably the only safe thing to do there."

Morgan scowled and started the Jeep. "Stop calling me Squirt."

Since Morgan was Morgan, he naturally wanted to explore around the house first. Since I'm Max, I would have preferred a couple lazy hours getting some sun on the dock and going back home. Since I have the most persuasive brother on the planet, we started off at the house—even though he promised not to go inside. We parked towards the rear of the house because the front wasn't that interesting; it was covered in saplings, and the windows looked like they were all blown out from the fire. Even after three decades, the soot stains from the fire were noticeable. I was relieved there didn't seem to be an easy way to get in the house from the front, because I had a feeling that was Morgan's plan.

On the backside of the house was a large terrace with a stone balustrade all around it, Morgan charged forward to investigate.

There was a large pool in the middle of the terrace. Strangely enough, it was rather clean and free of debris or water. I took a chance and offered a hopeful suggestion. "Are you ready to go swimming now?"

He didn't bother to answer me. Instead, he went to one of the doors on the terrace and tried to open one of them.

I grabbed his wrist. "What the fuck? I thought we agreed not to go in the house."

Morgan ignored me. He took the hem of his shirt and began to furiously rub the dirty glass. Then he peered inside. He was being entirely too quiet.

Unfortunately, his silence only piqued my curiosity. "What is it?"

He stepped away with a strange expression. "You should probably look for yourself."

I walked up to him and gave him a good hard push on the shoulder, because that's what brothers do.

"Asshole."

I chuckled and peered through the window. What I was seeing didn't seem right. The room seemed to be in perfect order. I'd been on a few of these expeditions in the past and abandoned houses were usually a mess. One thing I knew to expect was water damage, mouse droppings, and moldering furniture. The room looked like a maid cleaned it that morning. I stepped back and gauged my brother's expression. For the first time, he looked a little bit apprehensive. "Not so eager to go in there now, are you?"

Morgan put his hands on his hips. I knew his defiant stance well, because I was the only one he could use it with. Our parents would have locked him in our room for a week if he got that sassy with them. "We have to go in Max, this is now a mystery we have to solve."

"What if there is a deranged killer in there?"

Morgan huffed. "Quit being so dramatic, maybe it's an anomaly. The other rooms are probably in much worse shape."

"I'm sure that's what the guest said before Professor Plum hit him in the head with the lead pipe in the conservatory."

My brother laughed at me. "You are such a dork."

Morgan went to the next set of doors, there were six that opened onto the terrace. Thankfully he couldn't open any of them. I breathed a huge sigh of relief.

I let out an overly dramatic yawn. "Man, I could go for a nice swim about now and then about an hour in the sun." I looked at Morgan and smiled. "Doesn't that sound nice?"

"Where is your sense of adventure?"

I had a brilliant retort stored up for immediate use. "I don't have one because I actually listen to what Mom and Dad tell us. I'm pretty sure the only reason you've made it this far in life is because I've always been there to pull you back from doing something stupid." I poked his chest with my finger, "Like now…"

"You're never going to let me live down that time I tried to jump off the roof."

He was absolutely right because it was wonderful to have something to give him hell about. He was basically perfect when it came to everything else. "It makes sense actually, you got the math gene and I got common-sense." I clapped him on the shoulder. "It's worked well for us." It had too, I wouldn't have passed College Algebra without his help. Morgan took AP math all throughout high school.

Morgan ignored me, as he tended to do, and continued his exploration. There was one smaller door off to the side he hadn't tried. He had the tail of his shirt out again wiping away the dirty film on the glass. It was one of those doors with glass panes in the upper half, kind of like the back door of a regular house. He peered inside and reached out to wiggle the knob. The door opened and he was inside before I could say a word.

I went after him, there was nothing else I could do. I crossed my fingers and hoped for the best.

Morgan was standing in the middle of the kitchen. Thankfully there were plenty of windows so we could see. In retrospect, it might have been better if we couldn't, because it encouraged his sense of adventure.

The kitchen was completely spotless.

Morgan went to the refrigerator, one of those monster ones built into the wall. It was all stainless steel. There were four in total, I figured two of them were probably freezers. Morgan reached out and opened the door and the light came on inside.

The refrigerator was fully stocked.

I started to put my foot down, but all of a sudden, I was assaulted with a variety of images in my mind. I'd been in that very kitchen before—with the mystery guy in my dreams. We had done some naughty stuff on the butcher-block island. Most of the blood in my body suddenly rushed south. *I've seen this house before,* was the last thing I remember before everything faded to black.

Something was annoying the hell out of me. It was kind of like an insect that wouldn't stop buzzing around my face. I kept swatting it away and it kept coming back.

Then I heard a familiar, irritating voice, "Max! Wake the fuck up!"

Then my right eye was wrenched open. I could see my concerned little brother checking to see if I was still inside. I pushed him as hard as I could. "God, you are such a fucking pest! Leave me alone!"

Morgan ignored me and shook my shoulders. "Are you okay?"

When I started to remember, I let out a groan. "Dude, what the fuck happened? Why am I out here lying on the grass?"

Morgan hugged me. "Thank God you are all right!"

I sat up abruptly. "Morgan, what the hell happened?"

"You fainted."

Then I remembered to give him hell, I used my most vicious glare to help make my point. "This is why you need to fucking listen to me."

Morgan took my hand and pulled me to my feet. "Come on, we've got to get out of here. What if someone lives here?"

As he was leading me away, I asked, "How did you get me outside?"

"I carried your heavy ass."

I put my arm around his waist and pulled him into a bear hug. "Thanks man, I appreciate it."

"You should, because you are heavy as fuck."

We were silent most of the way home. I needed to tell him what I realized before blacking out, but decided it would be better to wait until he wasn't driving.

Unfortunately, it didn't take long for him to figure something was going on in my head, because I could tell something was going on in his. His forehead began to scrunch. I knew it was coming any second. I began my internal countdown: *three... two... one...*

"I'd like to know what caused you to pass out. You looked like you saw something."

There it was. I decided to be extra snarky. "I don't know, maybe it was the twelve pack of Cokes in the working refrigerator." I paused a beat. "I'm not sure, but I don't think they had twelve packs in the sixties."

Morgan nodded. "I admit it's weird, but you looked like you saw a ghost. I know you like Coca-Cola, but I'm not sure it would cause you to pass out." He turned and gave me a hard stare. "Let's hear it, Maxwell."

"Morgan, I've seen the inside of that house before."

The Jeep slowed noticeably. "Do what now?"

"In my dreams...You know the guy I've been telling you about...we did it on the butcher block island in the kitchen of that house."

Morgan wrinkled up his nose. "Max, you shouldn't have sex where food is prepared, that's gross. I hope you used disinfectant when you were finished."

I smiled. He seemed to be taking it better than I thought he would.

"Um Max, maybe we should go to the hospital. You might need a brain scan or something."

I knew he was messing with me, but I gave him hell anyway. "Good idea, I'll let you explain to Mom how I passed out in an abandoned house with a fully functional kitchen because I've been dreaming about having sex with a guy in there."

It didn't take him as long as I thought. "Max, we have to go back and take another look."

3

When we got back to our neighborhood, there was a large moving van in front of the house down the street. We slowed to investigate because it's a requirement for neighbors to be nosy. Dad was already onsite, doing his initial investigation, and flagged us down.

Mr. and Mrs. Conway were from Kansas City. I pretty much tuned out the rest because there wasn't anyone our age with them. I vaguely remember hearing something about one of them being an attorney.

Our neighbors were sizing us up and Mr. Conway asked the inevitable question, "Are you two twins?"

Dad always got a kick out of it and replied, "No, they're fourteen months apart." He was absolutely beaming because he was proud of us.

Morgan stepped away before Dad could ruffle his hair. Dad was already talking about how Morgan was their happy accident.

I was dejected because I wanted to meet neighbors my own age. I stood quietly and shuffled my feet, being polite as the Conway's exchanged pleasantries with our father.

The situation changed as a red Toyota 4x4 pickup pulled up in front of the house and a good-looking guy who appeared to be around our age stepped out. He was wearing a pair of athletic shorts, flip-flops, and one of those t-shirts with the sleeves cut off and open along the sides. Morgan and I had a lot of them. I hitched a breath because I could see his nipples.

I was disappointed because he wasn't the guy from my dream. He was a fairly big kid, maybe an inch shorter than Morgan and me and he had blond hair. I smiled because Morgan couldn't take his eyes off him.

He nodded politely at us and handed the bag he was carrying to his mom. "They were all out of the white rubbery shelf paper, I got clear instead."

Mrs. Conway inspected the contents carefully. "Good job, Nate, this will work just fine."

Morgan extended his hand. "Hi, I'm Morgan." He looked at me and frowned because I wasn't being polite enough for his taste. He elbowed me in the ribs. "This is my brother Max."

Nate shook his hand. "Hi, I'm Nate." He looked us over for a moment. "Are you two twins?"

Morgan exchanged the important biographical details with our new neighbor. Nate was eighteen and would be attending CU in the fall. Since I was already in college, he was too young for me. Nate was perfect for Morgan and didn't seem to mind being peppered with about a thousand questions. I knew they were going to be buddies when I heard Nate talking about playing quarterback in high school.

I was happy Morgan had a new friend and sad because Nate wasn't the one I was dreaming about. I decided I would scour the streets of Boulder until I found the mystery guy if that's what it took. I had a strong feeling he had to be somewhere in the area. It made plenty of sense to me because it wouldn't be any weirder than what we had seen already.

The house and my dreams had to be connected.

I must have spaced out because Morgan scowled and punched me in the shoulder to get my attention. He leaned in and whispered sharply, "What's the matter with you?" He grabbed my wrist. "Come on, he wants to show us his truck."

I was still plotting in my head, so I let him pull me along.

We learned that Nate's Toyota, his pride and joy, was a ninety-two model. It had a grey interior and a bench seat. The truck had big knobby tires with black wheels. It had one of those kick-ass pull-out Pioneer stereos with a CD player. Nate proudly told us how he installed it himself.

We ended up helping with the unloading because Dad was determined to show we were good neighbors.

Even though I was dejected, I had a nice time helping out and most importantly, watching Morgan and Nate interact. It was fun cataloging their differences. Morgan had always been gregarious and not afraid to talk to new people. I tended to be on the shy side myself and it looked like it might be a trait I shared with Nate. Every now and then, I could see Nate helping himself to a discreet glance at Morgan's ass, his chest, or the front of his shorts. It was cute watching them talk back-and-forth and check each other out. I knew it was going to be so much fun as I watched those two get to know each other—and I would tease Morgan about it relentlessly. Standard Operating Procedure.

We came to a large selection of gardening supplies in the moving van, along with a wheelbarrow. It made sense to put all the hoses and gardening tools in the wheelbarrow and take the entire load to the garden shed in the back yard. There was also a push mower. Morgan and I usually worked together seamlessly, so I took off with the wheelbarrow, assuming he would be right behind me with the mower. I stopped when I realized he wasn't following me. He was rooted in place, watching Nate carry a large box into the garage. I have to admit it was a nice view, watching Nate's muscles bulge as he carried the box, but I needed Morgan to get with the program so we wouldn't be there all day. I stood next to Morgan and could tell he had his eyes on Nate's ass.

I bumped him slightly with my shoulder.

No response...

I waved my hand in front of his face.

Nothing...

Since he wasn't paying attention, I decided on more drastic measures, I stood behind him and attacked his armpits with both hands. It was always guaranteed to provoke a reaction, because it was his most ticklish spot. As brothers, it was important to know those types of things about each other so we could make each other's lives as difficult as possible.

Morgan's arms immediately clamped down and I could barely move. Damn, he was strong. He couldn't stop the laugh from escaping, "Dude, quit playing around!"

When I got my hands back, I squeezed his shoulders. "Come on, get the mower, I want to get this shit unloaded and go home. You will have all the time in the world to stare at Nate's ass."

I knew my brother was hooked when he sighed. "Damn, it's a nice one."

The following week started out disappointing. Dad wanted Nate to work with us, but it wasn't going to be possible. Nate's parents didn't want him working with dangerous tools or toxic stains. Morgan was upset because he wanted to be around Nate more often. When my dad and my little brother were disappointed, guess who became disappointed by default?

Morgan was also irritated because it would be hard to find the time for any further exploration of the mansion. I have to admit, I wanted to do the same. The house became an almost irresistible draw because it was the only physical link to the mystery guy I was still dreaming about on a nightly basis.

Thursday morning was especially rough, our morning run kicked my ass particularly hard because I didn't get enough sleep the night before.

Morgan and Dad were already in the shop, and I was fresh out of the shower when I heard the doorbell ring.

I figured Dad had a package being delivered. He loved ordering the newest tool that promised to make our lives easier in the shop. I threw on a pair of clean running shorts and ran upstairs. I figured the

UPS guy wouldn't care if I was shirtless or barefoot because he would be more worried about getting my signature and getting to his next stop.

Our visitor wasn't the UPS guy.

My jaw hit the ground when I found myself looking into the expressive, chocolate-brown eyes of the guy I had been dreaming about for months. He was standing at my front door clutching a copy of the paper. He looked gorgeous with his dark hair and deep tan, nicely accented by his plain white, snug-fitting t-shirt. My gaze went downward to his flat belly and a nice bulge in his carpenter pants. He had on a pair of brown leather work boots that had seen a lot of use. I briefly considered asking him to turn around so I could see his ass. I shook the thought away and focused on his forearms with prominent veins and hands that looked like they were used to doing a lot of work. It was easy to imagine those hands on me because I had already dreamt it. I decided to focus on his face. He had such a nice one, what can only be described as classic good-looks. Mystery guy was able to say one word and one word only. "You…"

I nodded and smiled. "Hi, I'm Max."

He stood there staring at me for a moment and blinked a few times to make sure he was seeing straight. I was dying to know what he was thinking. "I'm Sam. I'm here about the job in the paper."

I was suddenly aware I wasn't wearing a lot of clothes. Sam's eyes were practically glued to my chest. "Um, why don't you come in? I'll get my dad, he's the one you want to talk to."

Sam nervously looked around the living room. "Should I wait here?"

I was becoming more modest by the second. If I didn't leave the room immediately my dick was going to be poking out the top of my shorts, because it was already starting to react. I was going to have to find an extra-long t-shirt. "Hang tight for a second, I need to get a shirt and some shoes." I grinned like a fool for a moment. "I just got out of the shower."

Sam looked me in the eye and pierced me with his gaze. "You don't have to on my account." Then he immediately flushed a deep shade of red.

I did too. I smiled as I ran down the stairs.

I threw on a shirt and grabbed my shoes and socks and ran back upstairs. The thought of Sam sitting alone in the living room was almost more than I could handle. I sat beside him on the couch and put on my ankle socks. His eyes were riveted on me. I put on my shoes and stood up. "Okay, let's go meet my dad." On the quick walk to the backyard where the shop was, I let Sam know my dad could be fairly intimidating, but he was fair. I couldn't help myself, I squeezed his shoulder and told him I was rooting for him.

We both jerked from the touch.

Dad was excited at the prospect of having some help in the shop. He sized Sam up quickly and took him to the patio for a proper interrogation. I smiled at Sam, as Dad led him away, to wish him luck. His smile, in return, promised we would be talking again, whether Dad hired him or not.

I had to give Morgan credit, he was nice enough to withhold his comments until Dad and Sam went outside. He looked up at me with a quirked brow. "Max, that guy is a grade-a hottie."

I nodded, still incapable of speech.

It was the only clue my super-sleuth brother needed to proceed. He got up in my face. "My big brother is smitten as a kitten."

My expression indicated it was much more than that.

Morgan studied me for a moment. He began to realize what was going on. "Holy shit! Is that the guy you've been dreaming about?"

I nodded slowly.

Morgan broke into a grin. "It's not hard to imagine taking that cutie in the kitchen after all. I'm not sure I would have been able to wait that long." He nodded his approval. "You have excellent taste, Maxwell."

My most immediate problem escaped my lips, "Morgan, what if Dad doesn't hire him?"

Morgan patted me on the shoulder. "Fear not, big brother, I will go and do my best to interfere."

I grabbed my brother and gave him a bone-crushing hug and kissed him on the cheek, "You are the best brother ever, Morgan."

I decided to keep busy after Morgan left because we had a lot of work to do, it was the best way to keep myself from going nuts.

Dad, Morgan, and Sam came back to the shop about twenty minutes later. They seemed happy and I was relieved. Dad introduced Sam as the newest member of the group; Sam was going to be working full-time for the rest of the summer. Morgan was practically doing a Snoopy dance, maybe we would have the time to do normal things that other people our age got to do. If anything, I would probably be motivated to spend even more time in the shop now that Sam was going to be around. If I did that, Morgan would have more time to spend with Nate because I could tell there was something special going on between the two of them. I wish I knew more, but Morgan wasn't being forthright with the details. It was kind of sweet of him to be that way, I knew he was being quiet so I wouldn't be jealous. Maybe he wouldn't have to work so hard at it now.

I was looking forward to talking to Sam a little more. He didn't come right out and say he was having dreams about me too, but the way he acted when I opened the door made it seem likely. I needed to know for sure and I was furiously thinking of a way to get him alone for a few minutes.

Dad gave me the perfect opportunity. "Max, I need you to give Sam a ride to his place so he can get his social security card. I need it for his paperwork."

He didn't have to ask me twice.

I learned a few things about Sam over the next half-hour. He had a car of his own, but it was currently in the shop. He had to walk to our house to interview for the job. We exchanged the usual details with each other on the way to his place. Sam and I were the same age and he'd been to college like me. Like dream Sam, actual Sam had a sexy southern accent, he was from Texas. He lived with his parents, who just took over an insurance agency in town. He explained they were living in an apartment because they didn't have the time to buy a house yet. I was looking forward to showing him around town.

Sam directed me to the parking lot in front of a decent looking apartment building. Before he opened the door, he asked, "Would you like to come in?"

I nodded, speech became suddenly difficult.

The two-bedroom apartment was neat and clean. I followed Sam to his bedroom where he had his social security card stashed in his desk drawer. I looked around the room because I was curious about what kind of guy Sam was. His bedroom was spotless. His twin bed had a cool green and blue plaid comforter. I couldn't help but notice the *Go Army* poster on his wall. I decided to mention it, because I couldn't imagine my dad would have had a conversation of any length with Sam and not mention he was a retired drill sergeant. "I like your poster."

Sam looked at the poster in question. "Thanks. I was in ROTC in Texas, I'm going to be part of it here too."

I was on the verge of exploding with happiness.

My eyes wandered to the other poster in the room for the University of Texas. "Were you a Longhorn?"

"Yeah," he frowned, "I was on the baseball team in high school, but I'm too small for college-level baseball."

A fellow baseball player was definitely a plus, it would help counter my football-loving brother and Nate. "It seems like we have a lot in common."

Sam looked at me with a smile. "Really?"

I was still being too much of a chicken to explore the biggest thing we had in common, but was more than ready to discuss the rest of it. "Yeah, we are both going to be sophomores and we are both in ROTC." I paused and smiled, "And, I played baseball in high school."

Sam's eyes lit up with excitement. "You play baseball?"

His expression made me happy. "I was a pitcher. I was pretty good, but I have to concentrate on ROTC because I got a scholarship."

He looked me over thoroughly before responding, "You look like you could throw a wicked fast ball."

I changed the subject because I was being shy. "Isn't football more popular than baseball in Texas?"

Sam shrugged his shoulders. "I guess I like being different."

I had the feeling Sam gave me an engraved invitation to get more information out of him, but I wasn't sure how to proceed. I had zero knowledge about how to ask the question I wanted to ask him the most. I decided to agree with him, "You could say the same about me."

Sam's gaze had sort of a laser-like quality after that. "You are in seriously good shape. Are you a runner?"

"Yeah, Morgan and I do Army-style PT every day, except Sunday, with our dad."

Sam put his social security card in his wallet. "That sounds fun, I like to run in the mornings. I need to step it up because ROTC was pretty tough last year."

I had the perfect solution. "You can work out with us every morning. Since your car is in the shop, I can come get you, it's not that far." I crossed my fingers behind my back, I was being awfully forward. For all I knew, he had friends of his own or another early-morning commitment. It was possible he didn't want to spend that much time around me since he was going to be working with us all day.

Sam's smile indicated my idea was a good one. "That would be cool." He sized me up once again, "I have no problem getting up early if I end up looking as good as you."

My shyness was practically strangling me, so I cleared my throat. "We should probably get going."

On the way back to the house, Sam put his hand on my knee. "By the way, we're going to discuss the dreams before the day is over."

I nearly ran into a telephone pole.

Sam laughed at me.

I was hooked.

Dad was highly impressed with Sam Rogers. He liked his attitude and his willingness to get the job done. He practically jumped for joy because Sam knew how to sand with the grain. When Sam showed up for the interview in his work clothes, ready to go, Dad decided to hire him on the spot. We started talking about PT in front of Dad, so he would hear, and he quickly decided Morgan and me could take turns picking Sam up until he got his car back.

Dad also liked how well Sam got along with Morgan and me. It was nice to see him relaxed and not having to wear his imaginary drill sergeant hat all the time. Having Sam with us that first day allowed Dad a little time to get out of the shop and have lunch with Mom. He needed a break now and then as much as we did.

The real training would start tomorrow because Dad had every intention of getting Sam familiar with all the power tools as soon as possible. Sam and Dad already decided he would work through the weekend since he started in the middle of the week. If Sam wanted overtime, which he did, Dad was more than willing to pay it.

Dad didn't blink an eye when I asked if Sam and I could hang out for a couple hours that evening. I was relieved it was going to be so easy for us to get to know each other without arousing suspicion. After a quick shower at my place and waiting a few minutes for Sam to do the same, we were on our way.

I decided to take Sam somewhere quick and cheap for dinner. Sam was in the mood for a Whopper from Burger King. A Whopper sounded pretty good, so that's where we went.

Sam took a big bite of his sandwich and a long sip of his Coke. He looked up at me while taking a drink because I was staring at him. "I think it's cool that you get along with your brother so well. I wish I wasn't an only child."

"You can borrow him anytime you want."

We made small talk while we ate. Sam was curious about all the places we lived since Dad used to be in the Army.

After Sam's last bite, he said, "Your dad seems pretty cool, he's not what I expected."

I nodded. "He's not as strict as you would think he could be."

"That's because you and your brother are trustworthy."

I could tell Sam was going to be special, his comment warmed me to my toes.

Sam checked his watch. "What do you want to do? We have about an hour before you have to get back home."

It really wasn't enough time have a long talk because if I wasn't back home by six, Dad would be pissed, even though I was an adult. Since I was dying to see the house again and gauge Sam's reaction to it, I gave Dad a call from the payphone outside the restaurant and begged him for a couple more hours. I was amazed when he didn't have a problem with it. Sam called his mom to let her know what he was up to. He told me she was happy he was making friends.

We were back in the Jeep moments later. I was getting nervous because we needed to discuss a few things.

Sam had a suggestion. "We could go for a walk or something."

I decided to take a chance. "Sam, there's a place I would like to show you. I have a feeling you might like it." I also had a strong feeling he was already familiar with it. "It's just a few miles from here, we should have plenty of time."

"Sounds good."

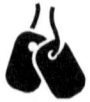

Sam let out a whistle when he saw the Buchanan Mansion for the first time. He scrunched his face in concentration as we got closer. "What happened here? Was there a fire?"

I gave him a brief rundown of the history as I pulled in the drive and headed towards the back of the house. It was around six o'clock, so it wasn't dark enough to be scary. I was hoping if we needed lights in the house they would be working. It was a reasonable assumption because the refrigerator was working the last time I was there. I knew I was taking several intuitive leaps, but I felt good about it, so I soldiered on.

Sam didn't seem frightened by the history and appeared eager to take a more detailed look. I knew Morgan would probably kick my ass for not bringing him along, but it was his choice to run out of the house like his pants were on fire so he could hang out with Nate.

Sam and I approached the back door where Morgan and I went in the last time. I stopped and turned towards him before we went inside. "If you don't want to do this, I won't be mad. We can always come back when it's earlier in the day or something."

"I'm good, Max. Let's check it out. I'm up for an adventure, this place seems pretty cool."

I asked one last time, "Are you sure? I wouldn't hold it against you, a lot of people won't go anywhere near this place."

"I'm not most people, Max."

Sam reached around me and opened the door. He eased around me and went in first after he took me by the hand. I was so happy, I didn't know what to do, except follow him inside, and not let go of his hand.

The kitchen area was just as it was when Morgan and I were there before. I showed Sam the refrigerator that was still fully stocked. Sam was a lot braver than me, he reached in and got a bottle of water, opened it and took a long drink. He smiled and handed the rest to me. "Here, have some."

Sam looked around while I finished off the bottle. When I finished, he appeared frozen in place. I sincerely hoped I didn't end up having to carry him outside. When I approached him, he turned and looked at me. "Max, I've seen this place before."

I hopped up and sat on the butcher block island. "You are having a much better reaction than I did the first time I was here," I took a minute or two to explain how Morgan had to carry me out after I fainted.

Sam walked over and stood in-between my legs. He didn't say a word, he took my face in his hands and planted the most amazing kiss imaginable on my lips. Things got pretty heated in a matter of seconds. After we parted, he stepped back. His eyes were at half-mast. "I've been wanting to do that all fucking day."

I wrapped my arms around his neck and gave him a kiss of my own. I reached down and gave his firm butt a good squeeze. "Do you want to look around? Morgan and I never got beyond the kitchen the last time."

Our hands were intertwined as we slowly and methodically explored the first floor. There was an immense dining room with seating for twenty, with an impressive chandelier that had to be worth a fortune. Sam didn't think much about it, he went to the switch on the wall and turned it on. The fact it worked was kind of anti-climactic.

There was a billiards room with a pool table, a bar, and several club chairs with low tables between them. There was a ballroom with a wooden dance floor and a wall of mirrors. Then we found the library with shelves wrapped around three of the walls with a huge fireplace dominating the fourth. All of the books were bound in leather and there were two ladders attached to a track by the ceiling that could be moved where they were needed. There were several lounge-like rooms, and a study with a fireplace of its own, a huge desk and several leather chairs. At the back of the house was the biggest room of all. It had a staircase of its own leading to an upper balcony with a beautiful view out the two-story windows at the back of the house. Sam and I decided to refer to it as the great room due to its size, the fireplaces at each end, and all the French doors leading outside to the terrace.

Sam opened one of the doors and we went outside on the terrace where we discovered another major surprise; the pool was full of sparkling clean water. The pond didn't seem like such a great place for skinny-dipping after that. It took everything I had not to strip naked and jump in the pool right there.

I could tell Sam was thinking the same thing, but he also wanted to see the rest of the house. Our hands were still linked. We weren't one-hundred percent sure that the house was a safe place to be, so we decided to keep close. It was a common symptom from watching too many horror movies.

In one corner of the great room was a doorway leading to a completely glassed-in room full of plants and trees. I knew it was called a conservatory because I toured several with my parents and Morgan in the past.

We decided to take the staircase from the great room up to the second floor. There was an even larger and more impressive staircase at the front of the entrance hall, but the smaller one was more convenient because it was closer. I shook my head at the ridiculousness of being in such a large house that we had to decide which set of stairs to take. The second floor was mainly bedrooms, but there were a couple of comfortable sitting rooms that looked like a great place to read a book. Each of the bedrooms, with an attached bathroom and spacious closet, were about the size of half a regular house. We counted a total of eleven different bedrooms upstairs.

Sam and I eventually wandered into a room that suited us the best, it had the most masculine decorating. The bed was huge, it looked like eight people could have slept there comfortably.

Sam took a seat on the edge of the bed and yawned and stretched dramatically. "Well, this has been fun, let's take a nap."

I moved closer. "We are so not going to be sleeping."

Sam leaned back on his elbows and kicked off his flip-flops. "What did you have in mind?"

I checked him out from head to toe, it was hard to decide where I wanted to start. I decided to go for the most obvious and got on my knees. He spread his legs to give me more room. The bulge in his shorts was getting bigger by the second. I reached out and gave it a squeeze. There hadn't been much chance to discuss our dreams yet, because we were so entranced with the house. I decided it would be a good time to bring it up. "I've sucked your dick dozens of times in my dream, I'd like to see what it's like for real."

Sam responded in the best way possible. "I've sucked you hundreds of times, I guess you better get busy and make up the difference."

I liked him even more after that, I had a deep unshakable need to be with someone who had a good sense of humor. I answered by pulling his shorts and underwear off. Sam's dick was hard and ready and I gave the tip an appreciative squeeze. It was the first time I ever had another guy's stuff in my mouth and it was wonderful. It was a little salty, but I liked it. I took as much of it in my mouth as I could and swirled my tongue all around it. Sam's hips lifted off the bed in appreciation and I managed to get both hands on his cute ass. I knew we would be doing this again.

I didn't have a lot of experience with what I was doing because it was my first time. I started to wonder in the back of my mind, how long it would take. I tried to make it as nice for him as I could by thinking about what I would like. I stopped a couple of times and gave his balls some attention. He wriggled in appreciation when I did, so I knew he liked it. When the inevitable conclusion came near, he started moaning and tried to push me off in warning, but I wasn't having any of it. I fully intended to see what he tasted like. Sam's orgasm was long and earth-shattering, he pulsed in my mouth several times. I happily swallowed every drop.

When he became conscious, he looked up at me and smiled. "That was fucking amazing!"

I was curious about something, and since I paid attention in my health class, I decided to ask. "Was that your first time?"

Sam nodded silently. It felt like such an honor to be his first. Since he was going to be mine, I couldn't wait to find out what it was like. I had overheard a lot of conversations in the locker room over the years. They all described blowjobs as the single best thing on Earth, I was ready to find out for myself if all the hype was true.

Sam and I traded places. Before he did anything, he looked up at me. "How about you? Have you ever had a blowjob?"

I shook my head. Sam grinned and went to town after that.

The guys in the locker room were spot on in their description, it was quite possibly the most wonderful thing I had ever experienced. Sam's mouth was warm, soft, and wet. It was the most intense thing I had ever had done to me. I knew there was a lot more that two people could do, I wasn't that stupid, but I wasn't in a great hurry. I felt like I had all the time in the world.

Sam crawled up in the bed with me and we made out for what seemed like hours. Rolling around on that huge bed with him was a lot of fun. We ended up making a big mess between the two of us because we got into rubbing against each other, I had no idea that could be so much fun.

All I wanted to do was curl up against him and fall asleep after that.

It felt like it might have been an hour later when Sam shook me. I learned I liked sleeping with him a lot.

I sat up abruptly. "Damn, we better get back, it's getting late."

Sam looked at his watch and frowned. He tapped the face several times. "That's weird, it stopped…"

I rarely wore a watch because of my highly developed sense of time, which was crucial with parents like mine. "Do you need to wind it or something?"

Sam shook his head. "No, it uses a battery. I guess I'll have to get it replaced." He huffed a bit, it was cute to see him so frustrated. When we were back outside, he checked his watch again and stopped abruptly. "That's too weird, now it's working."

We didn't think much further about it because we had been gone for a long time and I needed to get home. I didn't realize sex could make a person so sleepy. I didn't want to piss my dad off either.

On the way back to Sam's apartment I couldn't shake the fact that something didn't seem quite right, for one thing, it was still awfully bright out, considering how long we had been at the mansion. My internal clock told me it was getting close to when I needed to be home. In fact, my sixth-sense was crying *Danger! Danger! You don't want to be late!* The one thing that irritated my dad more than anything was tardiness. Drill sergeants are very precise when it comes to time and I didn't want to lose his trust. I decided to check the time one more time. "Sam, what time does your watch say now?"

"According to my watch, its six-forty-four."

It didn't make sense to me at all. If the time on his watch was correct, it was almost as if time had stopped while we were inside the house.

When we got to Sam's house, he jumped out. "Why don't you come in and we'll check the time? If you are running late, it might be a good idea to call your dad."

Sam's idea made sense to me, so I followed him inside.

According to the clocks in Sam's apartment, his watch was keeping perfect time.

Dad was surprised when I got home *early*. I told a little white-lie that Sam's mom needed him to run an errand for her and I decided to come back home. I earned some serious brownie points for not staying out later than we agreed. I needed to give what happened some consideration. I knew I would have to tell Morgan about it. It would be wrong not to, besides his finely developed intuition would sense it instantly.

I had enough time to take another quick shower. I decided the next time I visited the mansion with Sam, we would see if the house had working plumbing. It was risky to take another shower with Dad in the house because I was pretty sure he knew I took one before I left, so I made it a quick one.

When Morgan got home, I was stretched out on my bed reading a book. That was another benefit of having strict parents, we did a lot of reading. We had a TV in our room, but Morgan and I didn't watch that much.

I giggled quietly when Morgan rushed into the bathroom and the shower started. He might appreciate the ability to shower at the mansion too. I couldn't wait to talk to him about it.

Since I was eager to talk to him about it as soon as possible, and he barged in on me all the time when I was in the bathroom, I decided to return the favor. I poked my head inside the shower curtain, hoping to scare the hell out of him, but as usual, I didn't. When he saw me, he grinned lazily. "What's up, bro?"

I took a seat on the toilet so we could talk and Morgan could have privacy. I used my best imitation of Dad's voice to have a little fun with him. "Young man, do you care to explain the need for another shower? Are you trying to bankrupt us with the water bill?"

Morgan's head poked out of the shower. "Don't do that again, you almost gave me a fucking heart attack."

"I totally nailed his voice that time, didn't I?"

"Yes…"

I went out into our bedroom after that. I decided I could wait to talk to Morgan when he was finished. If I stayed in there and messed with him, he would end up using more water and we would have our dad on our case for real.

Morgan came out moments later. He joined me on my bed after he put a pair of shorts on. "How did the big date with Sam go?"

"We had a nice time. Let's talk about you and Nate."

Morgan's curiosity was in overdrive. "Why don't you want to talk about you and Sam first?"

Dammit, I was foiled again. I have always needed to learn how to control the conversation with my brother. "I took him to the house and something unusual happened."

He scowled at me for a moment. "You see, that's why you should've waited until I could go with you. Did Sam have to lug your heavy ass outside?"

I shook my head. "I'm surprised you didn't go to the house with Nate yourself."

Morgan shook his head. "I'm not sure he's ready for that yet. The place is kind of creepy."

I put my head in my hands. My brother was going to give me a headache. "Now you tell me."

Morgan patted me on the knee, his tone turned ominous, "Are you going to tell me what happened or do I have to start tickling?"

"According to Sam's watch and every clock at his apartment, time stopped while we were inside the house."

Morgan studied me carefully. "Okay…"

I looked up at him. "That's all you got to say?"

Morgan asked for all the specifics. When I was done telling him what we discovered, he looked up me and smiled. "I've heard of premature ejaculation before, but this is kind of ridiculous. Maybe you should work on your endurance before you two do anything again."

"I didn't say anything about having sex with him."

"Whatever, when Nate and I have a chance to mess around, we take it." He gave me his standard, *you're a dumbass,* expression. "Come on, don't deny you guys had some fun."

"How come you haven't given me any details about you and Nate yet?"

Morgan smiled at me. "We've been sucking each other's dicks like crazy. Is that what you and Sam did?"

"Yep."

Morgan stretched to pop his back. "What did you think of that?"

"It was incredible." I gave him my own special, *you're an idiot,* expression.

Morgan looked over at me and smiled. "That's nice to hear. Did the house freak Sam out? Were his dreams similar to yours? Did he recognize the place?"

"Yeah, when we were in the kitchen, he realized he had seen it in his dreams."

Morgan pinched my leg. "And he didn't even faint…"

"Come on… Are you going to give me hell about that forever?"

Morgan got out of my bed. "Come on, let's go upstairs and bother Dad. We need to do a better job of hanging out with him too." As I followed him out of our room, he stopped. "By the way, I think you and Sam should investigate every square inch of that house. It seems obvious to me that someone wants you two there for a reason."

The big question. Who?

July 1997

It was turning out to be a fantastic summer; Dad's woodworking business was getting a lot of orders, we were busy, and I got plenty of time with Sam. He did such a good job in the shop it was like Dad hired two people instead of one. Morgan was happy as a clam, because he got to spend even more time with Nate. I didn't mind taking up his slack because it meant more time with Sam.

We didn't have much opportunity to go back to the house, but we didn't mind because we were still getting to know each other. It was always nice when Dad needed to leave the shop now and then to get materials or bid on additional work. That allowed us little stolen moments where we could run into the house, or stay in the shop, and exchange an amazing kiss, sometimes even a blowjob—or three.

One of our main fascinations with the house, besides the time-altering benefit, was the possibility of going to the pool for a swim. We were planning to go on Sunday when we had more time.

It was during the week, when I had another vivid dream, the first since meeting Sam in person. This time around, there was a different guy. We didn't have sex. He was kind of hot, in a sixties sort of way, with his short, severely parted hair. I knew he was Jason Buchanan before he introduced himself, I remembered his picture from the article Morgan showed me when we did our research on the mansion.

His message was short and kind of cryptic. *If you would like to enjoy the pool with Sam, go into your closet now.* I groaned and rolled over, I was tired and not really in the mood to get out of bed. Jason became more urgent after I ignored him. *It wasn't a suggestion, Maxwell. Get your ass in the closet!*

Since I was raised to follow orders, I decided to listen. I frowned for a moment because I was in my underwear. I went for my shorts on the floor. I was trying to be quiet and not wake Morgan. Bossy Jason wasn't happy about the delay. *You certainly won't be needing those. Hurry up, I haven't got all night.*

I really would have preferred to be in my boxers instead of my briefs, but I didn't want to piss Jason off any further. I also needed to reinforce my preference for boxers over briefs to Mom so she would quit buying them. At least she didn't buy Spider-Man undies or something equally embarrassing. I thought about thumping Morgan on the forehead, because it was his responsibility to take care of laundry last week and he didn't get it done because he spent every spare moment with Nate Conway.

I crept to the closet door with my usual stealth and slowly opened the door. After I closed the door, I felt like an idiot because nothing happened. I was expecting a flash of light or something like the transporter on Star Trek. I huffed in irritation and decided to go back to bed. Morgan and I would share a good laugh about it tomorrow when I told him about it. He already thought I was nuts most of the time, so it would be a normal conversation for him.

I stopped in my tracks when I opened the door.

I wasn't in my bedroom anymore.

I wasn't in the Buchanan house either, I was standing in Sam's bedroom.

I stood quietly and watched him sleep. He looked yummy with the sheet kicked off to the side. He had one leg hanging over the edge and his head was buried under one of his pillows. I didn't feel so ridiculous about wearing white briefs because he was wearing a pair too. I decided they weren't so bad after all, because he looked hot in them. He looked like he might be having a dream of his own because he started to toss and turn.

Moments later, he sat up abruptly. He didn't seem too shocked to discover me standing next to his bed. He looked at me and smiled. "Looks like you and I had the same dream again."

I nodded and answered in a whisper. "The house seems to have another ability."

Sam got out of bed and took me by the hand. "Come on, Jason was pretty insistent about getting in the closet."

As he opened the door, I squeezed his ass. "I wonder if Jason is trying for some kind of metaphor with having us go into the closet."

Sam turned around, laughed, and kissed me on the nose. "You are such a goof." He pulled me inside, "Come on, let's go. Jason mentioned we could go swimming."

When we opened the door, we were standing in the bedroom at the mansion. There were a couple other curiosities that were hard to ignore; the bed had been tidied up from our last time and it was a bright summer day. It looked like it was about two in the afternoon instead of the actual time of two in the morning. I made sure to check the time before I left.

Sam looked around. "I guess if the house can stop time, it makes sense it could be any time of the day we want."

I nodded, "Yeah, nothing strange about that at all."

The corners of Sam's mouth quirked into a smile. "First one to the pool gets a blowjob!" He pinched me on the butt and took off running.

When I got to the pool, Sam's briefs were laying on one of the lounge chairs and I got quick view of his cute ass as he dove in the water.

It was a beautiful day for swimming. I'm not as good at estimating temperatures as I am with time, but it felt like eighty-five degrees. There wasn't a cloud in the sky and I could hear birds chirping in the distance. There was barely a breeze because I could see that the tall pines and the aspen groves were still.

We spent the next hour doing what guys our age do in a pool; we swam, we dove off the diving board, we dunked each other, and most importantly, I gave Sam the blowjob he rightfully earned for getting to the pool before me. We had a good time. The entire time we were there, we never heard a car driving by or a plane flying overhead. It felt like we were in a secure bubble somewhere. We could hear a lot of nature-related sounds; there were birds chirping and we saw several deer in the yard, who didn't seem bothered by the presence of human beings at all. They wandered through, nibbled some grass, and continued on their way in a leisurely manner. I wasn't entirely sure we were still in Colorado. Maybe that would have bothered some people, but I didn't give it much thought because I was with Sam.

After a long and tedious breast stroke competition, Sam and I were finally ready to get out of the pool. I smacked my forehead with my hand, when I discovered something we should have remembered. "We should have brought some towels from the bathroom."

Sam stretched out on one of the lounge chairs. "I guess we'll just have to air dry." He winked at me. "I think there's plenty of room for both of us."

We weren't too worried about being wet or dry after I joined him. We couldn't get enough of each other when it came to kissing.

When I woke up, Sam was on top of me, we were still in the lounge chair and we were nice and dry. I ran my hand down his back and squeezed his butt to wake him up. I was pretty sure we had dozed off for at least an hour. Apparently, falling asleep in the sun and not getting burned was another benefit of the house. It would have been nice to even out our tans, but I wasn't going to complain.

Sam finally came around to full consciousness, so we carried our underwear back inside with us. We went straight to the kitchen because we were thirsty. Sam and I shared another bottle of water and went back upstairs to our bedroom.

Sam looked me over from head-to-toe. "Are you ready to go back?"

Since his dick was at full-mast, I decided on the best answer possible, "No."

Sam rummaged through the nightstand beside the bed and happily produced a bottle of lube. He quirked a brow. "Maybe a nice relaxing hand job will help us sleep better when we go back."

I nodded with enthusiasm, "Awesome idea!"

We sat in the middle of the bed facing each other with our legs folded. Our knees were touching and we began to stroke each other after Sam put a drop of lube in each of our hands. I liked it, the lube was much slicker than the hand lotion Mom bought for us. I used my free hand to either play with his balls or tickle his belly button. It was cute to see him squirm and I was happy to discover a ticklish spot. If he ever gave me any sass, I knew how to get him back. I decided to check for others; I went for an armpit, but got no reaction at all. Sam's feet were within easy reach, so I reached out and slid my fingernails along the bottom of his right foot.

Sam practically flew off the bed. "Okay, stop…that's my super ticklish spot." His grin became slightly demonic. "If you want to keep playing this game, I'll be more than happy to start discovering some of yours."

I smiled, "Bring it, big guy."

I studied him some more. I couldn't help myself, I had to play with his toes, they were so cute. I didn't get the same reaction as before, I decided toes might not be off limits. I looked up at him for a moment. "I don't think I've ever noticed anyone's toes before, but yours are very cute." I gave them an appreciative squeeze.

Sam started stroking me with more enthusiasm. "You're just saying that because I sucked your dick."

I shrugged. "In fact, you are…" My words were cut off by one of the most mind-blowing orgasms of my life. I must have shot six feet in the air. I took a deep breath and sighed, "Holy fuck."

I pushed Sam on his back and began to stroke his dick with more authority. I also twirled his balls with the fingers of my free hand. Then I tickled the bottom of his foot again. Sam arched his back, but it wasn't because of the tickling, his dick erupted in white, frothy juice and shot in the air as high as mine did. He took a deep breath and let it out slowly. "Fuck, that was the hardest orgasm I think I've ever had."

I squeezed his knee. "I'm looking forward to giving you a lot more."

Since we were both a mess, we had the same idea. "I hope the shower works."

The shower was hot and had wonderful water pressure; apparently magic houses don't have low-flow shower heads. There was a bottle of shower gel and shampoo with a pine scent, so we washed every square inch of each other a couple times to make sure we were squeaky clean.

Once we were dry and had our underwear back on, Sam went back to the nightstand and began rummaging again. He pulled out two small bottles of lube and handed me one. "Let's each take one back with us for jerking off." He thought about it for a moment before he asked, "Do you think that would be considered stealing?"

I shook my head and laughed. "I don't think so. I have a feeling that's why those smaller bottles were in there anyway."

Sam took my hand, "Good idea."

We stepped in the closet and closed the door. Before we opened the door, I kissed him on the lips. "I'll see you later, hot stuff."

Sam returned the kiss, "Right back at you, stud boy."

When I opened the door, I was back in my room and Sam had apparently gone to his. I didn't have any time to think on it because I had a more immediate concern; Morgan stood in front of me with his arms folded across his chest. "Why are you in the closet at two o'clock in the morning?"

I had to think fast, I wasn't sure Jason wanted Morgan to know about the new express route to the Buchanan house. Thankfully, I had the bottle of lube in my hand, so I gave it to him. "I thought you might like this."

Morgan looked at me like I was from outer space and turned his attention to the bottle and briefly studied it. "So, you are telling me you got up at two in the morning because you remembered you had a bottle of lube stashed in there?"

I nodded and smiled weakly. "I was having a hard time sleeping because it seemed so important. We're brothers and brothers help each other out. I figured if I discovered something that helped the masturbation process, then it would be only right to share that information with you."

Morgan didn't seem convinced. "What's so special about lube? The lotion Mom gets us seems to do the trick."

Apparently Morgan and Nate had yet to discover the delights of water-based lube. "Hold out your hand."

Morgan did, so I poured a small drop in the middle of his hand.

He looked at it for a second or two, "That's not enough, numb nuts."

I stuck my finger in the middle of his hand and smoothed it around, so he could see it was. "You're gonna thank me for this."

Morgan pulled his underwear down and started to stroke in front of me. He had very few boundaries when it came to me. I was momentarily irritated to discover he was wearing *my* favorite pair of boxers, but decided not to let it show. He smiled at me. "This is awesome, Max. Thanks!"

"You are welcome." I made my way towards my bed.

Morgan joined me. I looked at him in alarm because he knew the rule. "Go back to your bed, Squirt. I'm not horny."

Morgan went back to his own bed. "Thanks, Max."

I was relieved I got away with it and Morgan was being quiet. I congratulated myself for my quick thinking, I finally discovered a way to avoid his questions! All I wanted to do was sleep, Sam wore my ass out.

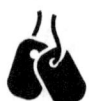

Sam and I decided to call our closets the *express route* whenever we made plans to use it, which we did frequently over the next few days. It was a time saver and Dad mentioned more than once that he appreciated how much work we were getting done.

Dad showed more appreciation a few days later. He handed me the keys to his truck, which I was never allowed to drive. "Why don't you and Sam go to the lumber yard and pick up an order for me?"

I swallowed nervously. This was a grand gesture on my dad's part. He didn't even let Mom drive his new dark blue Ford F-150, with an extended cab and jump seats in the back. I was pretty sure she didn't want to, but it still meant a lot to me. I studied him carefully to make sure he wasn't suffering from early dementia. "Are you sure?"

Dad nodded and smiled. "I think it will be okay, you and Sam are both adults."

"Thanks, Dad."

He patted me on the head. "You two go get some lunch first, the order will be ready in about an hour," he looked over at my jealous brother and winked at him. "We'll take care of things while you're gone."

Since Sam and I were now officially boyfriends, a distinction we made a few days earlier, I knew he preferred Burger King over practically all other restaurants in the world. Instead of asking, I headed for his favorite place. I actually liked Whoppers a lot, but still felt McDonald's had the best fries.

We had a leisurely lunch and didn't talk very much. I knew better than to try for Sam's attention when a Whopper was involved. I was beginning to enjoy his little quirks. We didn't really have that much to talk about anyway, because we spent about five hours at the house last night, and messing around wasn't the only thing we did.

Sam ate every last bit on his tray. He was idly picking up stray sesame seeds with the tip of his finger and eating them. He was too cute for words. I flashed him a quick grin, "Would you like me to get you a couple ketchup packets to go with your seeds?"

He smiled and stuck his tongue out at me. "Are you ready to go?"

I nodded. It was time to pick up Dad's order. I didn't want to be late, I loved driving his awesome truck.

We were back in the truck moments later. I started the engine and looked into the rear view mirror before backing out, just like Dad taught me. It was fortunate we weren't moving yet, because I let out a yelp when I discovered we had a visitor in the back seat.

Sam twisted in the seat to see what caused such a reaction. He was fairly calm considering that Jason Buchanan was sitting in one of the jump seats. Sam smiled and offered his hand in greeting, "Hi Jason, I'm Sam Rogers."

Jason shook his hand and grinned. "Nice to meet you Sam. You are a wonderful combination of cute and polite." He clapped me on the shoulder, "Isn't he, Max?"

I nodded because I was still too shocked to speak.

Jason let out a happy laugh. "I tell you what, it never gets old surprising people like that!" He squeezed my shoulder again. "Max, you had the best look on your face." He clapped his hands together and laughed in delight. "Sometimes this is a fun job."

I grimaced. "Just what I need, another smart-ass in my life."

Jason reached around the seat and poked me in the side, apparently he was a touchy guy. "Actually, that's why I'm here. We need to talk about a certain smart-ass and his boyfriend. I'd like to know why your brother hasn't brought Nate to the house yet, I want them to enjoy the benefits of the house like you and Sam have."

"Morgan is afraid Nate might not be ready to experience the house yet."

Jason was quiet for a moment. He looked up at the roof of the truck, it seemed like he might be having a conversation with someone we couldn't see. He took long enough that I started to worry about the time. "Don't worry about the time, I'll give you a few minutes so you aren't late." He gave me a wink, "Wouldn't want you to get in trouble with your old man."

Sam's brain had been functioning better than mine, so he took the opportunity for the obvious. "Are you a ghost?"

"Nope, I prefer to tell people I work Upstairs."

"Are you an angel?" I finally had enough wits to start asking questions.

Jason shook his head, "No, I'm just a minor, if not a little overworked, functionary."

"Can you tell us about Heaven?" Sam asked.

Jason shook his head again. "Sorry, it's against the rules to talk about how things work Upstairs." He smiled at both of us. "I like you guys. I like Morgan and Nate too. I want them to spend time at the house because it needs as much love as possible. That's the reason I'm here." He thought for a moment before he continued. "My superiors have given me the go-ahead to invite Nate and Morgan to the house.

For the first time, they would prefer you take them in your vehicle. If everyone Upstairs is happy, then I will go to them in their dreams and offer them the ability to jump from their closets." He squeezed my shoulder once again. "Would you be comfortable sharing the house and its wonders with your brother and his boyfriend?"

I nodded because I would never keep anything from Morgan. I started to speak, but noticed that Jason disappeared.

Sam looked at me for a moment, his eyes were wide. He summed the situation perfectly, "That's not something you see every day."

September 1997

Our perfect summer couldn't last forever. By the time it was over, Morgan and Nate were regular visitors to the house. The four of us didn't go out together that much because we were still pretty new at dating and liked as much alone time with our boyfriends as possible. We had a couple of late night swimming sessions where the four of us hung out and enjoyed the sunny weather. Thankfully, there were swimming suits at the mansion for each of us. Jason was a planner. We hoped the phenomenon would continue during the winter months as well, but we didn't know for sure. Jason wasn't very forthcoming about answering questions and only appeared when it suited him, which was basically never.

The four of us liked to take the RTD bus together each morning to campus so we didn't have to worry about parking. Sam and I shared ROTC, which was our first class of the day, and Morgan and I took one class together that he regularly gave me hell about. I talked him into taking a history class with me, so I could help him with his least favorite subject. Neither of us were happy to discover that *A History of Western Civilization to 1640* was the most boring class in the history of all classes. Morgan glared at me every time we walked into the lecture hall; that alone was worth the tedium.

Since Sam and I were still in the basic portion of ROTC, most of it was classroom instruction about basic military courtesy and traditions. The big stuff would start during our junior year where we would be a lot more active. Since we were in good shape, we weren't too worried about it. During the first two years there was an optional PT component and Dad encouraged us to take part. He reasoned we would be able to show our leadership abilities early on with helping out others who were struggling with physical fitness. Sam and I ended up making a few friends in the process, and the admiration of our instructors. The instructors, and fellow cadets, got a big kick out of the fact my dad used to be a drill sergeant and that I had to grow up with the most fearsome parent any of them could imagine. I let them hold on to their notions, even though my dad was basically a teddy bear who happened to be handy with a rifle.

Sam and Dad got along famously; Dad was impressed Sam was able to put in so much time at the shop and keep his grades up. Having unlimited study time at the house was turning out to be a big plus. As a matter of fact, I took an introductory engineering class my sophomore year because the field seemed an interesting direction to take, and the Army needed engineers. Dad was impressed and Mom was relieved. My only worry was how my folks would react if they found out about me and Sam, because at some point, they were going to figure it out. It was only a matter of time until Sam or I slipped up and said something incriminating, or one of my parents walked in on us sharing a kiss.

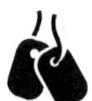

As the fall months progressed and the weather started getting colder, we moved our workouts indoors. I was starting to worry that Dad was on to Sam and me because I caught him looking at us from time to time. He never said anything, but it made me nervous. When I got especially worried about it, Morgan reminded me our parents had never said a disparaging word about gay people, or anyone for that matter. Dad wasn't one to discuss politics out in the open, so I had no idea if he was a Democrat or Republican. When Morgan and I turned eighteen, he handed us our voter registration forms and told us it wasn't his business which box we checked. I felt some comfort in how Dad never talked bad about people of color, so I hoped he wouldn't have a problem with me being gay. Sometimes Morgan was more worried than me, because he figured Dad would freak out over both of us being gay. I told Morgan he was more than welcome to tell Dad first since he was so worried about it.

Sam and I decided to take a stroll one Sunday afternoon. He enjoyed walking the Pearl Street Mall as much as Morgan and me. It was fun to get some exercise and get a bite to eat. Mom and Dad both warned me not to bring home any more incense because it upset their allergies.

There was a stand that sold crazy stocking caps and assorted hats. Most were too ridiculous to wear in public, but it was fun trying them on. Sam was cute as hell in the Marvin the Martian stocking cap, it stuck up in the air about two feet. I teased Sam about being taller than me for once. Since I was so funny, he gave me a hard punch in the shoulder.

Everything after that happened really fast. There was a blur as someone ran by. I did a double-take and pointed, "Sam, isn't that Nate?"

He looked in the direction I was pointing. "I think it is. Why is he running away?"

We got our answer a split-second later when two bigger guys ran after him. One of them shouted a slur that raised the hair on the back of my neck. "Faggot!"

There was no way my brother's boyfriend was going to get beat up when I was around, so I took off after them. I could hear Sam giving chase as well.

Nate and the others disappeared around a corner and we continued after them.

My heart sank when we turned the corner and I saw one of the guys had Nate pushed up against the wall. He was getting ready to do some damage.

I charged the guy like a bull and knocked him flat on his ass. I grinned because I was proud of myself. Unfortunately, his buddy wasn't too happy with the development, so he jumped me. I recognized him right away. Brent Sanders from high school. He liked to cause as much trouble as possible. We had exchanged words a couple of times. He drew his fist back and punched me in the face. "Well, if it isn't Nate's butt-buddy Max Carter!" He punched me again, before I landed a swift punch to his stomach.

Sam and Nate were busy taking care of Jake Anderson, the other guy. Between the two of them, they had him pressed up against the wall so he couldn't help Brent.

The police came and broke up the fight.

I knew I was in a world of shit when my dad came into the police station. I wasn't in trouble with the police because there were plenty of bystanders who heard Brent's shouted slurs. That kind of talk was frowned upon in "The People's Republic of Boulder." The paramedics had already seen to my eyebrow, which was split from the fight. It wasn't anything too serious, it needed a couple butterfly bandages. The police didn't want me walking home alone because they already sent Sam and Nate on their way once their parents arrived. Since Nate and Sam's parents weren't too sure of what was the real motivation for the fight, they decided it would be better for my dad to pick me up. They knew he was a strict guy, and they didn't want to be anywhere near the potential fireworks.

Dad stalked up to me and from the look on his face, he wasn't aware I was the good guy. "Young man, the police called and told me you were involved in a gay bashing. What do you have to say for yourself? Your mother and I did not raise you to beat people up. What the hell is the matter with you?"

"It's not what you think, Dad."

Dad looked around the room. "Where the hell is Sam? Wasn't he supposed to be with you?"

"He already left with his parents."

I didn't think it possible, but Dad was even more pissed. "Has he been filling your head with a bunch of anti-gay rhetoric? If he has, I'm firing his scrawny little ass tomorrow."

I laughed, which was a mistake, and made a bigger one because I wasn't thinking clearly. "Sam's ass is far from scrawny."

Dad's nostrils flared. "Are you mocking me? Just because you are in college, don't think for a minute I won't suspend every last one of your privileges." He shook his head. "I don't think I have ever been more disappointed in you."

I was in an official quandary; I could tell him Nate was the original victim of the gay bashing, but I didn't feel right about it because I didn't want to open up a can of worms for Morgan. If Dad found out about Nate, he would suspect Morgan was gay and it wasn't my place to tell him. I was going to have to be truthful though. I was a little more relieved about doing so, because my dad seemed pissed at the possibility I beat up a gay guy. "Dad, take off your drill sergeant hat for a minute and listen to me. I was defending myself."

Dad shook his head. "Maxwell James Carter...The police said you were involved in a gay bashing, how could you be defending yourself?" He was clearly confused.

I gave him an intense look until it sunk in.

I could tell when the realization hit. "Oh..."

I nodded. I kept my expression as neutral as possible because my full name had just been employed. When that happened, it was a clear signal that I was standing on thin ice.

"So Sam was with you and he helped you defend yourself?"

I nodded.

Dad smiled and grinned. "Well, that's better then." He reached for my hand. "Come on, let's get you to the ER, your mother will never speak to me again if I don't bring you in and let her make sure you are all right." He winked at me. "You have a pretty thick skull, but she will want to check for a concussion anyway."

"You aren't going to fire Sam are you? We need him and he needs the job."

Dad squeezed my shoulder. "No, I'm not going to fire your boyfriend. He's indispensable to both of us."

Our family meeting took place in the ER. Between Mom and Dad, it was impossible for me to keep Nate Conway out of the discussion. Mom and Dad were cool as hell about me being gay, but still found it impossible to believe that someone would have called any of us out for it. It didn't compute, so I had to tell them Sam and I were defending Nate. They had an equally hard time thinking Nate was gay too.

Dad went straight to the phone. "Morgan, I need you to come to the hospital. Your mother and I would like to have a conversation." There was a pause. I smiled as I heard the squawking coming from his end. "No, nobody is hurt or sick, just come here and ask for your mother like usual."

Morgan was concerned when he saw the bandages and my swollen eye. "You are going to have one hell of a shiner tomorrow."

Dad pointed to an empty chair, "Sit." He crossed his arms over his chest, the drill sergeant hat firmly back in place. His laser-like gaze focused solely on my little brother, and I felt sorry as hell for him. "Is there anything you would like to tell me?"

Morgan looked my way. I quickly mouthed the words, *They know...* I nodded at him in encouragement.

Since Morgan enjoyed poking the bear more than I did, he decided to have some fun. "Um, I think I got a b-minus in Calc."

Dad wasn't in a playful mood, he went for the door, turned and looked at Mom, "I'm getting a cup of coffee. Talk to these two idiots. I'll be back in ten minutes."

I looked at Mom, "Could you give us a couple of minutes?"

She smiled and headed out the door.

I told Morgan everything that happened.

He seemed to take the news well, even though I essentially outed him to our parents. He smiled at me. "Thank you for defending my boyfriend." He got up and hugged me. "I love you, Max."

"I'm sorry for outing you by default."

Morgan squeezed my hand. "It's okay, its time they knew. I'm tired of hiding."

I couldn't help myself, I laughed out loud. "We probably shouldn't say anything about the house."

"Dumbass."

When Mom and Dad came back to the room, Morgan and I had the distinct pleasure of answering some of the most embarrassing questions anyone should have to hear from their parents. Our folks were visibly relieved when we told them we weren't to the point where we needed condoms.

Mom left the room and came back with a shocking number of pamphlets about everything from STD's to the proper way to have anal sex. I was actually looking forward to reading that one, because I knew absolutely nothing about it, other than it would probably hurt.

Dad offered to take us to the store and buy condoms for both of us on the way home. We assured him we had enough money to buy our own and we would when the time was right. Morgan and I talked him into taking us to Dairy Queen for ice cream instead.

I called Sam to let him know I was okay when I got home. I gave him the full rundown. He was happy that Morgan and I didn't have to hide who we were anymore. He wasn't ready to let his parents know yet, because they weren't as progressive as mine. He told me he was gradually mentioning gay topics here and there to gauge their reactions. He thought it would be better than a dramatic coming out.

A terrible day became a good one and I was grateful because of it. I couldn't help but wonder if Jason Buchanan had anything to do with it.

I let the pamphlets Mom gave us sit on the desk for a few days before my curiosity took over. I already knew the basics from health class in high school. There were new treatments coming out for AIDS, but it was still something to be worried about. I felt I should be okay with what Sam and I had done sexually so far because he assured me I was his first. I believed him too. I had a strong feeling that there was no way he would be allowed in the Buchanan Mansion if he was a liar.

Morgan and I were in our bedroom one evening doing our homework. I finished with my history reading assignment before he did, so I decided to take a look at the pamphlets because the one about anal sex had me intrigued. The pamphlet was very explicit; it discussed how a person could do some of the preparation alone with their fingers and lubricant. My dick was throbbing in my shorts as I thought about it. That had never happened to me before because it wasn't something I gave a lot of thought to. In the past, most of my thinking on that matter involved doing it the other way around. With Sam in the picture, I wasn't so sure anymore. I decided it might be worth a try to find out since there was a bottle of lube in the bathroom.

Making up a proper story would be essential; Morgan was way too inquisitive for me to go in the bathroom and take a shower. I had already taken one earlier when we were finished working in the shop. I furiously searched for an excuse and finally came up with one that was completely bulletproof. I stretched and popped my back and let out a moan like I was hurting.

Morgan turned to me. "What's wrong?"

I did my best fake grimace and started to knead my shoulder. "My back and my left shoulder are killing me, I might have pulled something at PT this morning."

Morgan answered as I expected him to. "Take a hot bath, numb nuts, that's what we usually do."

I was relieved because he was engrossed in his reading and seemed completely unconcerned. Twisting his arm to take history with me was the idea of the century, he was so malleable. He didn't realize it yet, but he was taking another history class next semester.

I smiled as I went to the bathroom because he was muttering something about me being too stupid to live. It was a nice routine interaction—his curiosity wasn't piqued. I figured I had a good thirty minutes of alone time, I needed it because I was hard as a rock thinking about what I was about to do.

I got the water nice and hot, but not very deep. I soaked for a few minutes, because I was still a little sore from all the pushups that morning. My white lie was the best kind because it was partially true. I was looking forward to calling Sam so he would meet me at the mansion if my experiment worked out.

I was surprised when I found out it felt fantastic to have my finger in there. It was kind of like scratching an itch I couldn't get to. It didn't hurt at all. I had no idea my dick could get any harder, but it did. I used my free hand and a little more lube to do something about it.

I was having a pretty good time when the door flew open and Morgan came in carrying a plastic bag. "Go away, I'm kind of busy here!" It was the best thing I could come up with considering I had a finger in my ass and was jerking off.

Morgan smirked and pulled a dildo out of the bag and handed it to me. "Here, give this a try, I think it will be a lot easier than your finger."

I sat there dumbfounded.

My brother smiled. "I knew you were reading the pamphlet, Max. I got one for you and me because I'm curious about it too. I wouldn't be a very good brother if I didn't share."

At least he didn't want us to use the same dildo.

I looked the dildo over carefully. It wasn't huge, as a matter-of-fact it was *Sam-sized.* I smiled at Morgan, "Thanks, you are the best."

Morgan sat on the toilet. "Okay, go ahead and try it out."

"Get out of here and I will."

Morgan shook his head. "I paid $30 for it, I should at least get to watch."

"I have a couple twenties in my wallet, you can have them." I shooed him with my hand.

Morgan surprised me when he left the room, it was a clear sign he was really getting into Nate.

The dildo was a lot more fun than I thought it would be. I slid it in and my dick got twice as hard. Instinctively, I began to stroke. Within a couple of minutes, my toes curled in anticipation as a zinging sensation began to radiate from my lower spine. I hitched a breath as my dick erupted in a gusher of white, ropy strands. It was nice to know that giving myself to Sam wasn't going to kill me.

Morgan came back in as I was drying off. He was completely naked and he pushed me out the door. "Go away, it's my turn."

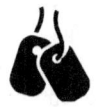

Sam had no idea what was waiting for him when he joined me at the Buchanan house. He got to the mansion seconds after I did.

I stood there watching him as he came out of the closet. As usual, he looked good enough to eat. I gave him a smile. "Hey, hot stuff."

Sam gave me a hug and a long kiss. When he finished he stepped back. "You smell good. Did you just take a shower?"

I nodded and decided not to over-share.

"Aw, that's sweet."

I kissed him on the forehead. "I missed you."

He laughed, "You are such a goofball, we saw each other a couple hours ago." He ran his hands along my sides. "Damn, you look good."

I ran my knuckles over his stomach, which had started to get really nice. I liked it before when it was flat, but now his abs had become more defined, which I enjoyed even more. "All the working out you have been doing with us is starting to show." I stuck my finger in his belly button. "You are going to have a six-pack in no time."

He squirmed a little before he answered. "I've gained eight pounds since we met."

"All that exercise and Dad's breakfast burritos will do it."

"I'm going to have to have him show me how to make those, they are awesome."

I filed the information away, I would make sure Dad taught me first; Sam was the kind of guy I wanted to cook for. My finger began to trace downward from his belly button, "If you ask him to show you, he will be the happiest guy in the world." I didn't really want to talk about my dad's cooking skills. Since I was in the mood, I tried something that wasn't my usual thing, because I had always been afraid of pissing Sam off because he was smaller than me. I wrapped my arms around him and picked him up.

Sam put his arms around my neck, his big smile and flushed skin let me know he wasn't mad. "This is kind of nice."

I kissed him some more and carried him over to the bed and set us both down, so he was nestled in my lap. I reached up and ran both thumbs along his eyebrows. "What do you think about trying something new?"

Sam reached down and squeezed the tip of my dick. "I'm pretty sure anything with you is going to be great." He swallowed nervously. "I'm game for whatever you want to try."

My hands slid to his hips. "What would you say if I asked you to fuck me?"

"Seriously?"

His confounded expression made me laugh. "Why does that surprise you?"

Sam's cheeks turned a healthy shade of red. "I thought you would want it the other way around."

"Why is that?"

He looked a little embarrassed as he shrugged his shoulders. "I don't know, maybe because you are bigger? You are definitely more of a stud than me."

He was being ridiculous, but I could see where he was coming from, so I didn't give him a hard time about it. "I don't think size has anything to do with it." I squeezed one of his cute toes. "I think it would be amazing to get nailed by the cutest guy in town."

Sam kissed me on the nose. "Max, going to the next step is a big deal. I'd like to know how you feel before we do this."

I knew what he was getting at, so I let him know the absolute truth. "Sam, I've never been in love before, so I don't really know how it's supposed to feel." I checked his expression for a second before I continued, he seemed to like what I said so far. "I'm pretty sure that's what I'm feeling, there is no way I would do this with anybody else."

I don't think Sam could have squeezed me any tighter, his arms and legs squeezed me until I could barely breathe, "I love you too, babe."

Once we recovered from using the l-word for the first time, there was a quick discussion about condoms. There were a few in the drawer, courtesy of Jason. I trusted Sam with my life, so I had no problem going bare with him. I could tell he had no intention of playing around from his earlier comments. We decided not to use them. There was some comedy when I mentioned Mom's pamphlets and Morgan's gift because he wanted to know how I figured it all out. I could have lied and said something about researching it on the Internet, but Sam was someone I wanted to be truthful with.

Sam was all about sticking his finger in my ass while giving me a blowjob, he encouraged me to do the same with him too because he wanted to see what it felt like. We ended up in a sideways sixty-nine and from the blowjob he gave me, I could tell he was having a pretty good time with my finger too.

When it was time, I had Sam sit on the edge of the bed. I stood in front of him and eased myself down onto him, using my hands on his thighs for leverage, I sucked in a breath as he penetrated me. The real thing was a lot more intense than the dildo.

Sam wrapped his arms tightly around me as he peppered the back of my neck with kisses. His words of encouragement were amazing, "Max, I've never felt anything so awesome in my life. I am so happy that I'm doing this with you."

I felt tingly all over and it wasn't from having his dick in my ass. I started to move up and down, I couldn't believe how hard my dick was, I put a small dab of lube on it and started to stroke.

After a couple minutes, Sam squeezed my hips. "Let's try a different position."

I let him position me the way he wanted. I ended up on my back with Sam standing in front of me, he lifted my legs up on his shoulders and entered me again. He gave me a big smile. "This is much better, now I can see you."

I stretched out and put my arms behind my head and let him do the work. He was stroking me as he pounded away. I couldn't get over how good it felt.

The familiar dull ache of impending orgasm started to build. It felt like little jolts of electricity were shooting out of my fingers, my toes, and my dick. My ass began to involuntary clamp down on Sam as my orgasm started to build.

Sam sucked in a breath, "Holy fuckballs!"

I smiled because I couldn't have said it better myself. My back began to spasm and my dick started to spew.

Sam let out a loud groan and thrust three more times, much harder than before. He accentuated each thrust with, "Oh. My. God!"

I felt the same way.

We weren't able to move for at least five minutes. Sam leaned down and kissed me while he was still inside. I pulled him down on top of me and squeezed his sexy butt and kissed him some more.

We took a quick shower once we got ourselves together. When we were dried off and back in our underwear, I wasn't quite ready to go home. "I'm thirsty, why don't we go down to the kitchen and have a Coke?"

There was no way to repress my laughter when we stepped into the kitchen. Morgan and Nate had the same idea, but it had nothing to do with something to drink. Morgan was on his back on the butcher block island with his legs on Nate's shoulders, getting a good pounding of his own.

Sam was so cute, he turned into me and put his head on my shoulder. I knew he wasn't embarrassed because he was laughing his ass off.

Poor Nate looked like a deer caught in the headlights.

Morgan let out a loud groan. "That's it, I'm asking Jason to put a refrigerator upstairs!"

I couldn't help but state the obvious as I made my way to the refrigerator. "Nate, you have a really nice ass." Since I enjoyed tormenting my brother, I took my sweet time. I got a couple of glasses with ice, instead of drinking out of the can like I usually did, I also poured the contents of both cans into the glasses right on the island next to Morgan so I could prolong the torture.

Morgan grabbed a glass and took a big drink of it. "Max, you are such a dick sometimes."

I patted him on the stomach and stuck my finger in his belly button. It was his ticklish spot too. "Be nice, I just made it last longer for both of you." I looked down at Nate's dick, which was still inside my brother and nodded with approval. "Dude, you got a nice big dick too." I squeezed Morgan's shoulder, "Way to go, Squirt."

Sam and I decided to snuggle on the couch. There was a bit of a chill in the house. We were both in just our underwear, so it was kind of fun to use our shared body heat to keep warm.

"You know, if you two are chilly, all you have to do is turn on the fireplace."

We nearly jumped out of our skin when we heard Jason's voice.

He was on his knees behind the couch with his chin resting on the cushion; his head was in between ours, inches from both of us. When I turned, I could see his mischievous expression.

Jason let out a chuckle. "Ha-ha, I got you again! It's way too easy to scare the shit out of you two, I almost feel bad when I do it."

I scolded him immediately. "Why don't you ever answer when I call for you?" I gestured to Sam and my hand stayed on his knee because I liked touching him. "We have a lot of questions."

Jason stood and walked around the couch and sat on the floor in front of us. "Unfortunately, I can't answer a lot of them, but since I'm free for a moment, I thought I would give you a few pointers about the house so your time here will be more comfortable."

Sam, who was always sweet and thoughtful, voiced a legitimate concern. "Shouldn't we wait until Morgan and Nate are done so they can hear this?"

Jason snickered. "Um, they're going to be a little while yet. They decided to go another round." Jason gave me a stern look. "I expect you to tell your brother what you've learned today."

I shivered, it seemed even colder than before. "Of course, just tell us already. I'm freezing!"

"It's very simple," Jason explained, "just tell the house what you want."

Sam must have been colder than me, so he tried first. "Turn on both fireplaces."

Each fireplace at opposite ends of the room immediately sprang to life.

"You can also tell the house what temperature you would like," Jason offered helpfully.

"Seventy-four degrees," I said.

The house was instantly warmer by several degrees; I think it must have been about sixty-five before I had said anything.

Jason had another example that fit in with what we already knew. "Warm summer afternoon."

It was suddenly a bright sunny afternoon and the temperature in the house adjusted automatically.

Sam tried a different approach, "Winter blizzard."

The view out the windows changed accordingly. Sam and I both got up to look out the windows at the howling, nasty weather outside.

When we sat down, I blurted out the first that came to mind. "Turkey sandwich on white with bacon, cheddar, and ranch dressing." I smiled when a silver plate with the sandwich appeared in my hand. It was cut in two so I gave half of it to Sam.

Sam took it and smiled. "Thanks babe, I was starting to get hungry."

Jason beamed at the two of us. "Aww, you two are so sweet." Then he reached in his pocket as he looked at Sam. "I understand you have a birthday coming up next week."

Sam nodded. "I'll be twenty."

Jason smiled and handed him a joint. "This is for you, in case I don't see you before the big day."

I was surprised to say the least. "You smoke pot in Heaven?"

"We like to refer to it as Upstairs, Max." Jason smiled and winked. "Maybe you should try some yourself, the stick is still lodged pretty firmly in your ass." Jason grinned before he gave us another revelation. "There's a nice side benefit to consuming marijuana here at the house, when you leave, it will be completely gone from your system." He waggled a finger, "Be sure not to overdo it and as a safety precaution, I'm the only one who can bring it into the house." His stern gaze became softer, "You are welcome to an occasional beer, but please stay away from hard liquor until I let you know."

Jason, Sam, and I shared a hit off the joint.

Jason stood, as if he was ready to leave. "Oh, before I forget. I would appreciate it if the four of you could be here midnight on Christmas morning, I have a few things for you and my superiors have decided I can give you a more thorough briefing about the house and why the four of you have been chosen."

Before I could speak, he was already gone. I looked at Sam. "Dammit, he always leaves right when I have another question."

Sam smiled and took another bite of his delicious sandwich. Then he gave me a smile full of heat, "I want you to fuck me before we go back."

He would never have to ask me twice for that.

Late 1997

The holidays were upon us. Thanksgiving was two days away and I was facing an unfortunate reality; Sam and his parents were going back to Texas for four days. Sam and I weren't terribly worried because of the mansion's magic, but we weren't sure how long distances would come into play.

There was another reason I wanted to know if we could travel to the mansion from afar; Sam and I were going to have to spend a few weeks of our summer after our junior year in Fort Lewis, Washington as part of our ROTC commitment. The experience would be a lot better for us if we still were able to share unlimited time at the mansion. I tried my best not to dwell on it too much. It would've been nice if Jason would have answered more of our questions, but he didn't. That was going to have to wait until Christmas.

I was doing well with my engineering class, it looked like I was going to get a b-plus. It was hard to tell with college classes because so much of the grade depended on finals.

Morgan and I didn't spend a lot of time discussing my future as far as the Army was concerned, he preferred not to talk about it at all.

The one thing that made me sad when I thought about it was the prospect of not having him around as much. That was one of many reasons why it was important to know if I could make it back to the mansion if I was far away.

Nate and Morgan were both happy, they seemed to have the least complicated relationship of all. Nate's parents eventually found out about his relationship with Morgan and it didn't bother them one bit. It was really nice because our parents started hanging out with each other too.

Sam's parents finally found a house they liked, but they weren't going to be able to move in until the first of the year. Sam was excited about moving into a bigger space where he could have a bedroom in the basement like the rest of us. He hoped he would be able to have more privacy and that it would allow me to spend more time with him. We enjoyed spending time together in the real world too. For the most part, his folks seemed pretty cool. Of course, nobody had parents as scary as mine.

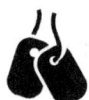

Thanksgiving turned out fine because Sam and I were able to see each other for hours at a time while he was in Texas. That, more than anything, helped me realize we could have a relationship with each other no matter where we lived or what we were doing. I worried less about the future and enjoyed the time I spent with Sam.

Morgan and I surprised our parents when we informed them we wanted to go to the Christmas Eve service at St. John's Episcopal Church. We didn't think Jason would mind us being a little late.

Because of Jason and the house, church seemed like something we should check out, although Jason had yet to say anything about organized religion. Morgan picked the church because he had done the research and the Episcopal Church was friendlier to gays than many of the others. Our parents weren't religious, but believed in God, so they let us go by ourselves. They understood it was something Morgan and I wanted to do on our own.

We were going to have a packed house for Christmas dinner later that afternoon; Mom and Dad invited Nate's parents along with Sam's. Mom has always been a good planner, all she had to worry about was the turkey and ham and the others would bring the rest. Morgan and I were alarmed when she first told us about her plans, but were relieved when she assured us she would make her famous carrot cake from scratch.

Family was important, but the best part of the holiday for me was when Morgan, Sam, Nate, and I met at the mansion after the church service. Jason was waiting for us and he'd clearly outdone himself with the preparations. The great room of the house was beautiful with multiple Christmas trees and garland everywhere. It wasn't snowing outside for real, but he made sure it was for us. There were also presents under the tree.

The delicious smells of dinner held most of our attention. Jason smiled as he ushered us into the dining room, all laid out and ready. The table was covered with a holiday feast; turkey, ham, and about a dozen other side dishes. I knew I would have to add an extra mile or two to my morning run over the next few days because we would be having a second huge meal in a few hours.

Jason sat at the head of the table and Sam and I sat on one side with Nate and Morgan on the other. Each of us had a glass of red wine, Jason picked his up and offered a toast. "Merry Christmas to all of you, thank you so much for spending this time with me."

We returned his sentiment and had a sip of Pinot Noir, which Jason explained was excellent with turkey. He was amused that none of us liked it that much.

We spent a few minutes loading our plates and exchanging normal dinner conversation, much of it insults between Morgan and me. He always took more than his fair share of the mashed potatoes.

Jason obviously wasn't ready to start giving up any details yet, so we enjoyed our meal and the companionship of our friends. About an hour later, after we were done and he snapped his fingers to clear the table, he snapped them again for pumpkin pie and hot coffee. It was impossible to live in Colorado and not like coffee, because there were shops on every corner.

I was the first to prod Jason into speaking. Since we had a fairly snarky relationship, I decided it would be the best approach to get the conversation started. "Okay Buchanan, start talking, we're ready for some details."

He loved to mess with me. "I might be persuaded if you behave."

Sam took over. "What's with referring to Heaven as Upstairs?"

Jason started off as cryptically as usual, or he wouldn't be Jason. "It's basically a joke. The proper term would probably be sideways instead of Upstairs, if you really think about it."

There were four sets of knotted brows staring at him in confusion. "Guys, Heaven is a human religious term. It's against the rules to favor a specific religion because there are so many." He let that soak in for a moment and continued when he saw we weren't going to be getting into a major discussion on theology. "Think of your existence on Earth as a hologram you are looking at straight on. If you tilt it sideways, you can see the image change to something you didn't fully realize before. The realm I inhabit can see earth—or the entire universe for that matter—differently than you can."

Since Morgan was a dork, he nodded first in agreement.

Just for good measure I called him out, because it's my place as the older brother to do so. "You are such a nerd."

Morgan agreed with me. "Yep, the same one who bought you a dildo so you could learn how to please your boyfriend."

Jason's eyes bugged out of his head for a moment, then he laughed out loud.

I gave it right back to him, "You certainly seemed to appreciate my idea about having sex in the kitchen."

Jason was still giggling and snorting. "You guys are so much fun, I really missed a lot being an only child."

"You can have him," I offered hopefully.

Sam squeezed my leg. "Max, it's not nice to keep offering to give your brother away." He was amused too.

Morgan was shocked. "You've offered to give me away before?"

Nate was the quietest of the group by far, but he was laughing too. He kissed Morgan on the cheek. "I'll take him in a heartbeat."

Sam had questions and he was determined to start asking them after the laughter settled down. "Jason, what's so special about this house?"

"It's a long story," Jason began, "but I'll condense it down to its most basic elements so we aren't here for hours. The story starts thousands of years ago when native peoples inhabited this area. The Indians had a civilization of their own, living in harmony with nature for centuries before the Spaniards started exploring and settling the area. As the United States grew, more and more white settlers moved in. Some of the native customs were abhorrent to the new arrivals, especially the way they embraced homosexuality."

I think it became a little clearer to us why we were sitting in the house.

"I've heard about this kind of stuff before," Sam said.

Jason nodded. "The Spanish settlers murdered anyone who displayed homosexual behavior. At the site where this house was built, a male couple was part of a local tribe. They held an honored position in their society as wise-men who could treat illnesses and communicate with spirits. The Europeans felt they were in league with Satan and had them dismembered." Jason shuddered. "Their remains were fed to the dogs."

Nate's eyes were wide as saucers, "How do we fit in with all that?"

"We hope the four of you will help with the solution." Jason held up his hand as the four of us began talking at once. "Guys, there is more for me to tell you. When something like this happens, the people I work for notice. A geographical area is officially declared to be stained after a hateful act. As a result, restless earthbound spirits became attracted to the area. That is why this house and its grounds are rumored to be haunted."

"Why don't the spirits affect us?" Morgan asked.

Jason grinned. "Because the four of you have a pass from Upstairs. Restless spirits won't interfere with you as long as you are protected."

I shook my head. "We are here because of what happened hundreds of years ago? Why do we deserve all this?"

"There were two additional incidents at this location beyond what happened to the Indians," Jason explained. "Because of that, the stain is even greater."

I looked at him with all the compassion I could muster. "One of those was you, wasn't it?"

Jason nodded. "I know you have read about what happened with me and Rick. The news reports at the time didn't mention we were intimate with each other, because no one knew." He frowned before he spoke again, "Let's just say that Rick had some issues with guilt." Jason stopped and leveled his gaze at Morgan. "I'll go ahead and move to the next chapter that relates to this property." His eyes flashed with playfulness, "I'll do my best to keep it simple because I know you have issues with history."

Morgan immediately looked at me in an accusing manner. "Asshole!"

I held up my hands in surrender. "I haven't said a word to Jason about your favorite subject."

I could tell he wasn't really mad at me, but it didn't stop him from giving me the middle finger. "You are such a dick sometimes."

Jason shook his head at our antics. "As you can imagine, this area was attractive to new settlers. The mountains and their snow packs provided ample water for towns and cities to grow. The weather isn't too bad, so people started moving here. Before my ancestors bought the property about a hundred years ago, there was another family that farmed this land. There were four people in the family; a husband, his wife, and their two sons. The sons weren't gay, but they discovered masturbation and their father caught them enjoying themselves together in the barn." Jason shook his head sadly. "The father strangled both of them to death for violating the laws of nature."

Sam was incredulous, "Wait... Guys weren't even allowed to jerk-off back then?"

I squeezed his leg in support because we were lucky to be living in more reasonable times.

Jason shook his head. "No, they weren't... and especially not together."

I looked over at Morgan, who seemed equally horrified. What we did from time to time could have gotten us killed back in the day. Jason's story made sense to me. Since I'm the son of military parents, I phrased my question in terms I understood the best. "The people Upstairs drafted you because of what happened to you here in this house."

Jason nodded. "And that's why I'm here."

"What do we need to do to make the stain go away?" Nate asked.

Jason smiled at all of us. "That's the easiest part of all. The four of you need to love each other and spend as much time as you can here at the house. Since the four of you have been coming here, the stain has already gotten smaller. I think after the four of you share many happy years under this roof, it will go away completely."

Jason looked upward at the ceiling. It looked like another conversation we weren't party to. We were used to it, we had seen it before. After a moment, his gaze returned to the four of us. "Guys, I'm going to have to go pretty soon." He stood up and went towards the great room. "Let's open the presents and I'll let the four of you get on with being boyfriends and enjoying the house."

The gifts weren't extravagant, but they were nice. I had already gotten Sam a couple of CDs and I thought he would probably be giving me something similar. We were trying to keep it simple and not spend a bunch of money because we already had everything we wanted.

I knew Sam really wanted a leather jacket and he knew I wanted a new pair of orange running shoes we saw at Gart Sports. Jason had come to all of us in a dream after Thanksgiving and told us not to go all out because he wanted to get something nice for each of us. Sam was happy to get the jacket and I was happy for my new shoes because my others were worn out. Nate got a bottle of his favorite cologne and a watch. Morgan got two gifts as well, the first was a gag, it was a book on the history of Colorado. Morgan got to use one of his favorite words and called Jason a dick because of it.

Jason howled with laughter.

Morgan's other gift was a new camera, which was timely, because he broke his old one, and Mom and Dad had no intention of buying him another one. I decided I would take the blame and tell them I got it for him if they started asking questions. It would also provide a valuable opportunity to remind my little brother that I'm not a dick.

Each of us gave Jason a hug and a kiss on the cheek. What he did was very thoughtful, considering everything he had already done for us.

Jason bid us a Merry Christmas and promptly vanished into thin air.

The four of us were alone in the great room…

Morgan was the first to say something. "What should we do now?"

Sam had an idea right off the bat. We hadn't told Morgan and Nate about the little wooden box on the wet bar that seemed to have a never-ending supply of marijuana in it. Sam went to it and pulled out a joint and waggled his brows at the rest of us.

Sam took a hit and passed it to me.

I took a big hit and held it out to Nate. "You want some?"

"I probably shouldn't. If my parents found out, they would ground me for life."

I looked at Morgan before I responded. I could see the wheels turning in his head and was surprised he hadn't said anything, I turned back to Nate. "That's the best thing, if you smoke it here, it only affects you when you are in the house." I smiled happily. "When you leave, you aren't stoned anymore. Isn't that awesome?"

Nate reached for the joint at once, "Gimme."

Nate passed it to Morgan, who was still giving me the stink eye.

I acted in the usual manner. "What's up your butt now?"

Morgan huffed dramatically. "Is there anything else you have neglected to let us in on?"

Sam was starting to get pretty good at dealing with my brother. "Jason paid us a little visit the other day when all of us were here." He cleared his throat. "You two were a little busy in the kitchen."

Morgan turned slightly red, but still felt spunky. "And then you conveniently forgot to tell us."

"We're telling you now," I offered.

Morgan took a hit off the joint, but he still wanted details. "Okay, we have pot at the house. Anything else we should know?"

I ran him through a quick demonstration of adjusting the temperatures, turning on the fireplaces, and changing the outdoor weather. I showed him how to ask for things to eat and gave him a slice of pumpkin pie. "Here, this is for you, your blood sugar might be getting a little low." I smiled happily, "You tend to get a little mouthy when that happens."

Morgan had a special way of his own to test what he learned, I suddenly felt a cold shiver down my spine when I saw the gleam in his eye as he spoke his request with special flourish. "Everybody naked!"

I glared at my brother as we were all buck-naked on the couch. "You are such a perv."

Sam decided to intervene, "Hot summer day."

Then we went skinny-dipping…

9

June 2000

Even though we had the benefits of slowing time at the mansion, the real world moved on when we went back to it. Before we knew it, our sophomore and junior years were finished. Sam and I were scheduled to leave in a few days for the four-week Leader Development and Assessment Course at Fort Lewis, Washington. We were excited to finally be able to learn about battle tactics instead of military courtesy or how to march with a wooden rifle. When we got back, there would be one more year of college, we would graduate as second lieutenants and go to an Army school for our career specialty. Sam and I were both taking engineering courses, we hoped it would help us stay together.

One afternoon Dad sent Morgan to get supplies. He gestured for us to take a seat on the stools in the shop, it appeared we were going to get another lecture, Dad had been handing them out freely for months. "I have something important to discuss with the two of you."

I groaned. "Dad, I hope you're not going to give us the talk about being gay in the Army, that's about the only thing you haven't talked to us about yet."

Dad's piercing gaze shut me up. "I wasn't going to get into that, but since you brought it up…"

Sam looked at my Dad and then he smiled at me. "Thanks for bringing up the issue, Maxwell."

Dad laughed at Sam's impression of his drill sergeant voice. "You guys have done an admirable job at being discreet." He shook his head, "I'm not sure how you do it, but if you keep acting the way you do, I don't think either of you are going to have a problem serving in the military."

Sam and I shifted uncomfortably, we weren't about to tell him about the mansion and how it was the primary reason we were able to control ourselves. Thank goodness for our magic closets. I smiled at my dad and deployed my full arsenal of flattery, "You have taught us well. Before we do anything rash, we step back, take a deep breath, and look at the big picture."

Dad shook his head and rolled his eyes for good measure. "Even though my bullshit meter is pinging, there is actually something else I wanted to talk to you boys about today."

Sam and I were happy for the subject change.

Dad continued like he didn't notice, "The Leader Development and Assessment Course is a very big deal, you two are going to have an intense month. As the name implies, the Army will be assessing your leadership abilities, and I wouldn't be a very good father, or former member of the Army's Training and Doctrine Command, if I didn't let you know about a couple of important details. Since the two of you played baseball in high school, you are familiar with the way colleges send out scouts to offer athletic scholarships."

Sam and I nodded—even though we weren't good enough to receive a baseball scholarship at CU, we were happy with the way things had worked out so far.

Dad continued, "There will be officers representing career specialties in need of good leaders. They will be watching you closely. I know both of you have expressed an interest in engineering, but if you do really well and impress those who are watching you, you could be offered something more interesting."

"Such as Special Forces?" I asked hopefully.

Dad always got happy when I mentioned the possibility of being a Special Forces officer. He nodded slowly. He never gave his official endorsement, because he didn't want Mom to find out. "Yes, please remember the Army always needs good combat officers, especially in the Infantry. It's important for both of you to do your best and impress as many people as you can." Dad looked at us closely and smiled. "I'm absolutely certain both of you will be able to do that."

I've always enjoyed ruffling my dad's feathers, and I had an excellent opportunity to do so again. "I assume you are going to dispense a few nuggets of wisdom to help us dazzle those who are fervently searching for the next generation of Army leaders?"

Dad took a deep breath and rolled his eyes. "You know, I've always thought your brother was the biggest smart-ass between the two of you, but I'm not so sure now." He gave me a second eye roll for emphasis, "Your mother and I talk about this all the time and I enjoy letting her know it comes from her side of the family."

Sam was laughing too, he enjoyed our exchanges. Sometimes, if he was especially brave, he would add some special commentary of his own.

Dad became serious, "First of all, neither of you should be worried about offending your fellow cadets. You are training to be officers where independent thought is essential. If you have an idea or suggestion, don't be afraid to give it. Quick thinking is what the assessment teams will be looking for." His expression became a bit sterner, "This will be extremely important with any tactical exercises. We've had two years to talk about battle doctrine, so you have more than enough information to make a contribution. I will be very disappointed if I find out you two aren't the first to raise your hands and talk intelligently about tactics."

Sam and I nodded like a couple of five-year-olds.

I was almost certain Dad had someone who would be reporting back to him about our training. Dad seemed satisfied, so he went on. "I also have crucial advice for your first day. One of the first exercises we put new trainees through is the Duffel Bag Experience. When trainees are issued their gear, they are instructed to put everything in the duffel bags. Before we leave the reception battalion for our basic training units, we have everyone put their duffels in a pile on the parade ground. Then we have the troop transports pull up and order all the recruits to find their bag within five minutes and assemble in formation." Dad smiled at what was probably a fond memory, "It is exceedingly rare for a new platoon to achieve the goal." Dad gave us an especially pointed stare, "We also use the exercise to look for potential leaders, we like to pick out the first round of squad leaders and the platoon guide from those who help the others and show leadership potential."

I nodded in understanding. "They will be doing something similar?"

"You can bet on it."

Sam and I knew better than to ask what we should do. Dad was clearly expecting us to demonstrate our leadership potential right there.

Sam spoke first. "I would start picking up bags and shouting out names."

His idea went along with what I thought. "I would also tell the first few people to set their bag aside where they can get to them quickly and to start calling out names in an orderly fashion."

Dad smiled at both of us and nodded like he was impressed. "I think my work here is done. Why don't the two of you get out of here and get some ice cream or something?"

Sam and I had a better idea, we went to the mansion.

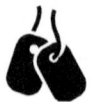

Our relationship was beginning to change in subtle ways. We were completely familiar with each other and started looking for new ways to keep it fresh and spicy. Once I discovered my boyfriend had a competitive streak, all bets were off.

One of Sam's favorite things was to have me jerk him off. Hand jobs tend to be underrated because there are so many other things a couple can do. Not Sam, he almost always liked for me to jerk him off before we started in on anything serious. He explained it helped him take the edge off. Since we were both young, it usually took us about five minutes to recover. On those rare occasions it took longer, we swam, because we had all the time we wanted.

Sam liked to spread out in front of me with his ass in my lap. It was his invitation for me to stroke and he liked to wrap his legs around me. Watching him come unglued was my favorite pastime. He had a hard time explaining why he liked it so much, other than how good it felt. It was always a lot of fun to explore his ticklish spots while I was doing it; right in his belly button, or the bottom of his foot. Sometimes I would prolong the experience for over an hour by bringing him almost to the point of release before I stopped. It drove him completely nuts. It was fun to make him beg.

One time, while I was stroking him, I casually issued a challenge. "There is no way you can last more than sixty-seconds." I felt pretty good about it, he was already writhing and squirming in need.

Sam smiled. "Oh, you're on!" Then he thought about it a little more and grabbed my wrist. "Wait, what happens if I can't?"

I was happy to share the details because I'd been plotting the scenario for days. The wheels started turning in my head when I got a good look at my brother after he stepped out of the shower last week. His abs were looking better than mine and naturally, I demanded to know why. I had a six-pack that I was proud of and Morgan had the beginning of an eight-pack. He informed me in his matter-of-fact way, that when he was with Nate at the house they did more than have sex—they liked to work out too. Let's just say they discovered a unique way to make it a lot more fun. I have always hated crunches, so I was more than ready to try something different.

Once Sam asked, I appeared to think for a moment, even though I already had it worked out. "Four-hundred crunches if you lose."

Sam groaned. "You would suggest something like that. What if I win?"

"Then I'll do four-hundred crunches."

Sam looked at me for a moment and nodded. "I have a feeling there is something you aren't telling me…"

I squeezed the tip of his dick and smiled. "Of course, it wouldn't be as fun if I didn't." I slid my hands under his ass cheeks, lifted him up and gave his balls a good licking before I continued. "I can assure you it will be the most entertaining workout you ever had."

Sam wrapped his legs around my midsection. "I guess you better get stroking then."

Sam set the timer on his watch as I slowly began to stroke his cock. I always got such a kick out of watching his facial expressions when I had his dick in my hand. I reached down and twirled his balls to let him know how cute he was.

He grabbed my wrist. "That's not fair, I'll never last if you do that."

I chuckled because I didn't really care how it worked out anyway, I figured we would both be doing plenty of crunches before the day was over.

I could always tell when Sam really got into it, he started to thrust in my hand. I was happy to see he was on the verge of losing it. Then the timer on his watch went off. I was shocked he won my challenge, so I promptly stopped and left him in bed alone.

Sam was indignant. "Hey, what the hell? I didn't even get off!"

I wiped my hands on a towel. "Don't worry, you will get your chance." I arched a brow and turned for the bathroom. I cackled as I walked away, "Eventually."

"Bastard!"

Going down the stairs was kind of fun. Sam made me carry him since I didn't get him off. He was starting to seriously enjoy it—so was I.

Sam looked confused when I carried him into the dining room. "Why are we going in here?"

I put him down and pulled out a chair. "Here, have a seat."

Sam looked at me like I was crazy. When I sat down in front of him with my legs under the chair, he began to understand what was going to happen. He eyed me carefully as I got on my back and scooted a little closer to the chair after performing some quick geometry in my head, "I have a feeling I'm going to like this."

I did my first sit-up and smiled. "Yes, you are." Then I went down on his cock before going flat on my back again.

Sam was about to burst by the time I hit a hundred-and-fifty, so he pulled his right foot up and made me suck his toes for the next ten revolutions.

That bought us a little time, he didn't give me a mouthful until two-hundred-twenty. I stopped for a moment because I had to savor his delicious seed—and my stomach was killing me.

Sam smiled and shook his head. "Huh-uh, you made a challenge, you have to keep going until you're finished. There's plenty for you to lick and suck."

Just to drive him crazy, I teased his sensitive belly button with my tongue for five crunches. By the time I got my four-hundred in, he came in my mouth again.

In all, it was not a bad way to get in a workout.

Sam let me recover for a couple of minutes before he stood up. "That was awesome! What do you want to do next?"

I groaned. "I think you're trying to kill me."

Sam chuckled, "We could do something less strenuous if you want."

The sound of a clearing throat stopped our discussion in its tracks. Jason was calmly sitting at the head of the table, completely unconcerned with our nakedness.

I immediately covered myself with my hand.

"I'm sorry if I dropped by at a bad time." He clearly wasn't.

Sam turned the chair around and took a seat at the table, which hid his business from view.

I stood up and did the same.

Jason took pity on us and snapped his fingers. Suddenly, we were wearing our swim trunks. "I can only stay for a moment. I have something new for you to try out since you will be at Fort Lewis in a few days." He sensed we were thirsty, so he snapped his fingers and three Cokes on ice appeared in front of each of us. Jason picked his up and took a long drink. "Delicious, they only have Pepsi in the machines upstairs."

We laughed at his look of disgust.

He continued, "Since there aren't many closets for the two of you to go into at Fort Lewis, I have been given permission by my superiors to allow a more efficient method to reach the mansion. Starting today, you can travel either way by mouthing the word, 'Shazam.'"

We giggled at his sense of humor and grew quiet for a moment.

Jason's expression was somewhere in-between concern and amusement. "This would be a good time to try out what I just told you."

Sam and I snapped out of it, we were still recovering from the ab workout. I had a valid concern, "If we try it now, will you be here when we get back?"

"Guys, I'm running short on time."

We hadn't seen him in months. I knew Jason preferred humor in our interactions, so I decided to give him some. I shook my head dramatically. "It's a good thing your superiors don't send out surveys."

Jason slapped the table in amusement. "Good one! Try out what I told you. I'll be waiting when you return."

Sam and I turned to face each other and mouthed the words in unison.

I appeared back in my room in my bed. I mouthed the word again, and I was instantly back at the dining room table. Jason was sitting there as promised and Sam appeared a split-second later.

Jason grinned. "It's always a relief when it works as advertised, much better than searching all over Peoria."

Sam and I had a quick deliberation. We had several questions stored up for the next time Jason appeared. Sam wanted to go first, but I felt I deserved to go first, since I had to do all those crunches. He laughed at me and motioned for me to ask my question. "Jason, how come you never mention religion?" It was the one question we wanted to know the most.

Jason stood up. "Well, it's about that time…"

Sam jumped up out of his chair. "Come on!"

"I didn't say I would answer any questions, I only agreed to be here when you got back."

I tried to reason with him. "Jason, we haven't seen you since last Christmas. It's weird how you want to celebrate Christmas with us but you never talk about the Bible or anything remotely religious."

"Did you not appreciate the presents I got for you?"

"Yes." Sam answered.

"Maxwell, did you not appreciate the running shoes I got you?"

I lowered my head and shuffled my feet. "Yes, I wore them every day until they wore out."

Jason smiled and snapped his fingers. Two new pairs of running shoes appeared on the table. "Consider these a small gift of my appreciation." He cleared his throat, "I'm sorry guys, but I'm not allowed to answer more questions. We have rules and it would be bad for me to break them." Jason's expression turned into the same one my dad used on me when he was trying to make a point. "If I break the rules, you could end up having to deal with someone that doesn't have as good of a sense of humor as I do. I will let you in on one little tidbit, I haven't been around as much because the four of you are doing a good job at loving each other and reversing the stain that has been on this area. This house is not my only responsibility. I've been very busy for the past couple of years with a troublesome little town in Indiana." He looked towards the ceiling. He was obviously being told something. "Gentlemen, I have to go, good luck with the training."

Jason was gone before we could say a word.

Sam went over to examine our new shoes. He held up his pair. "Sweet! They have purple stripes!"

Mine had green stripes and I loved them too. It was nice of Jason to give them to us, we went through running shoes like you wouldn't believe.

Sam set his pair down on the table and backed me up against it. He kissed me on the chin. "I guess it's my turn to do some crunches now."

July 2000

Dad's description of the Duffel Bag Exercise was spot-on. Sam and I did exactly what we said we would; we stepped up and tried to impose some order on a chaotic situation. Although it took seven minutes for the platoon to get in formation, Sam and I felt good about what we did.

There were a few cadets pissed at us for ordering everyone around, but learning to do so was our ultimate purpose for being there. I think their attitudes softened after we got to run three-miles in our combat boots for not following instructions.

Since Dad had lectured Sam and me frequently about what to expect, we were handling it nicely. The Leader Development and Assessment Course was basically an abbreviated version of Basic Training that the Army used to train enlisted soldiers. Many of the basics that were taught in the first half of Basic Training, such as military courtesy, learning the phonetic alphabet (alpha, bravo, charlie…), and basic first aid procedures. Since all of that had already been covered, the primary focus of the course was operating in the field, along with rifle and grenade qualifications.

Our first half of the course saw us living in a camp environment, if you have seen M*A*S*H on TV that's what it was like. All of us got to take part in loading up the tents and riding to the campsite where we assembled our camp as our first task. Most of the cadets stayed in twelve person tents while the instructors and commanders enjoyed smaller four person tents. We had a command tent as well as a dining tent that doubled as a classroom. The only permanent feature on site was the latrine.

One of the primary goals during the first half of the course was qualification with the M-4 rifle, the hand grenade, and quick demonstrations of other weapons like the Squad Automatic Weapon (SAW), grenade launchers, and the shoulder-fired anti-tank weapon. Everyone had to qualify at the marksman level for both the rifle and grenade or they would have to go through the course a second time.

Dad was right about all the observers. Of course there were our instructors, but with most of our exercises there were always two or three people standing off in the distance watching and writing in their field notebooks. On our first day, I saw a grey-haired lieutenant colonel writing in his notebook when Sam and I took charge and tried to get everyone to work together with the duffel bag exercise.

That wasn't the only time either. A few days later, we were conducting a map-reading exercise. Sam and I could tell right away the instructor was using the wrong coordinates, which would have put us on the wrong side of the river we were moving towards to set up a fixed position, Sam and I called him out on it and our names got written down again.

Sam and I also made some new friends during the first couple of days. Troy Atherton went to Fort Hays State University in Hays, Kansas and Dane Cooper attended the University of Oregon, in Eugene. They were both hoping to be Infantry Officers and they seemed to be the ones who always agreed with us when we made an observation. They were the first to help with the duffel bags and they were the first to agree when the instructor misread his map. I had a feeling the lieutenant colonel was writing their names down as much as ours.

Most of the cadets in our group were in good physical shape. Troy and Dane were the ones who most closely matched our level of physical fitness. The four of us were never worn out after a run or any of the other PT we had to do. They were also smoking hot; Troy was shorter like Sam, with a similar lean and muscular build. He had light brown hair that seemed to be turning blonder by the day, and he had cute freckles on his nose. Dane was almost the same height as me, and every bit as built. He had more chest hair than the rest of us combined. I teased Sam about it privately, because I'd seen him looking a time or two.

I ended up spending a lot of time with Troy because we were assigned as buddies at the beginning. Sam got to do the same with Dane. There was no way they were going to allow Sam and me to be buddies together, because we were from the same school. It was important for the cadets to network and collaborate with people from other parts of the country.

Troy and I got to pull an all-nighter during our first week in the command post. All we had to do was receive hourly reports from the cadets on guard duty and those in the observation post (OP). We were by ourselves and it was one of the first times we could talk freely.

The night was about halfway over when Troy sat down beside me after he logged the latest check-in. "There's something I would like to ask you."

Uh-oh.

I had a feeling I knew what the topic of conversation was going to be. Over the past few days, I was getting the feeling Troy might bat for the same team Sam and I did. I decided to act nonchalant about it. "Sure, what's up?"

He cleared his throat quietly. "Are you and Sam together?"

His question was fraught with danger. Dad had cautioned Sam and me about this very thing; he told us about people in the Army who would act friendly, only to report their findings at the first opportunity. I didn't get that vibe from him, so I asked him a question in return. "Is there something we've done that makes you think we are?"

"Not anything that anyone else could see."

His answer implied he had gaydar, so it seemed okay to be more open. "We have been together since May, 1997."

Troy shifted in his seat. "I think that's awesome."

"Thanks…" I couldn't help it, I had to ask. "So…"

Troy's laugh was cute, even when restrained. "Looks like we're batting for the same team, Max."

Sam and I kicked ass on the rifle range. Dad had prepared us well, he had no intention of being embarrassed if *his boys* couldn't shoot a rifle. He had an old AR-15 he used to train us on. He took us to a local rifle range and we kept going until he felt comfortable we knew what we were doing.

Dad's training paid off. We got the opportunity to help several of the cadets strip and clean their rifles to Dad's exacting standards. The instructors were impressed and our names were once again written down.

Sam and I qualified as experts our first time out. As a result, our names were added to another list and, instead of sitting around doing nothing, we got to help those who needed more one-on-one time.

Sam and I behaved ourselves for our first two weeks. We were too frazzled to even think about going to the mansion because we were in unfamiliar surroundings outside our comfort zone.

The rifle range was a chaotic and busy place, so we eventually had a moment to ourselves when the next group moved in to take their positions to qualify. On our way back to where the rest of our platoon was assembled, Sam gave me a slow smile. "I think I'm going to stop off at the latrine now that I have a chance."

It was like an engraved invitation, so I returned his smile. "Suddenly I need to pee really bad."

We didn't have to use the restroom and since we were alone, we mouthed the magic word and we found ourselves standing on the terrace at the mansion. When we got there, Morgan and Nate were using the pool.

Morgan noticed us the second we appeared and he flew out of the pool on an intercept course. His greeting was so enthusiastic, he nearly knocked me on my ass. "God I've missed you!" He pushed me back with his hands on my shoulders. "You look good too!"

I laughed. "It's only been a couple of weeks, Squirt."

Nate came out of the pool to greet us too. His greeting was only slightly more formal. He gave each of us a long hug and a kiss on the cheek. "You guys got here at just the right time for a nice swim." He wrinkled his nose, "Or a shower."

I grinned because I knew we didn't smell that good. The shower tent wasn't one of our favorite places, plus we had been in the hot sun all morning. "Let us get our swim trunks and we'll join you."

Morgan had a better idea. He shucked off his trunks and we went skinny dipping instead.

For the most part, my brother didn't like to talk about us being in the Army. Morgan wasn't exactly a pacifist, but he wasn't enthusiastic about the prospect of Sam and me serving either. I was pretty sure most of it had to do with us being apart, more than anything else, so I was surprised when he started asking us questions about our training while we were at the pool. "Are the two of you finished with Basic Rifle Marksmanship?"

His question surprised me enough that I fell off the pool float. It was a bad idea trying to share it with Sam anyway; it didn't have enough displacement to adequately hold both of us. When I surfaced, the others were laughing at me. Sam was laughing the hardest because he was stretched out and comfortable, so I turned it upside down and threw him off too. There was the obligatory struggle and I had to wrap my arms around my boyfriend to keep him from prevailing. I was doing a pretty good job, but his bare ass was wriggling against me and driving me crazy. More than anything, I wanted to go into the house and have some alone time.

Morgan paddled over on his float. "Are you planning on answering me?"

I let go of Sam and smiled at my brother. "Of course…" Then I threw him off his float for good measure. Nate was the smart one, he was seated at the edge of the pool and stayed out of it. When Morgan surfaced, I gave him a broad smile. "Thanks for asking, we both qualified…" Sam cut me off when he dipped underwater and gave me a blowjob. "Oh my God…"

Morgan was aware of what was going on, so he decided to be a pain-in-the-ass. "I'm sorry, what was that again?"

"Experts…Morgan…We qualified as experts!"

Morgan nodded appreciatively. "Nice!" He looked down in the water at Sam doing his thing and arched a brow. "He definitely has impressive lung capacity."

Alone time with Sam, at least in the short-term, wasn't going to be on the menu. Morgan had been pestering me for months about having a group activity and I promised we would, but I kept putting it off. I didn't think Morgan was a pervert or anything like that, he just wanted to see me and Sam go at it. His reasoning kind of made sense since Sam and I got to watch Nate nail him that day in the kitchen. He accused me of enjoying it because I took my sweet time getting a Coke from the refrigerator, which I freely admitted. Besides, it was hot watching Nate pound away on him. Morgan was determined to talk about it again. It was kind of hard to argue with him after looking over at Nate, who was hard-as-a-rock.

All of us were.

I still wasn't sure what Morgan's dirty little mind had in store for us, so I decided on a time-out. "I'm going inside for a Coke, I'm thirsty."

I went ahead and got four glasses out and filled them with ice because I knew the rest of the crew would be in the kitchen any second. As they filed in the kitchen, I could see they were all still hard. I poured the rest of them a drink because I had always been polite. I was starting to think Morgan had a good idea. Sam and I had been together for quite a while and it was always nice to find a way to add a little variety. I watched Morgan drain his Coke. "Since this is your idea, what do you have in mind?"

Morgan thought about it before answering. "I don't know…Maybe I could top Nate and you could top Sam right next to him." His cheeks flushed red.

I reached out and played with my boyfriend's dick. It seemed happy with the idea, so I smiled at Sam. "What do you think?"

Sam shrugged his shoulders. "I don't know…" Then he grinned and pushed Morgan hard in the shoulder. "Seems kind of anti-climactic for such a famously dirty mind. Your big brother usually likes a challenge of some sort." Then he reached out and started playing with my dick too.

Nate looked at Morgan and smiled. "Have you told them how we do pushups yet?"

Sam and I both groaned at the same time. We'd had plenty of exercise already.

Sam reached out and played with my business again. I knew what he was in the mood for by the way he'd been acting since we stepped into the latrine. I think he was more interested in the first proposal. I picked him up because I knew he liked to be carried when he was in that type of mood. He wrapped his legs around me. I looked over his shoulder at Morgan and Nate. "Looks like the first idea is the winner." I carried him out to the great room.

When Morgan and Nate came into the room, Sam was already giving me a blowjob. Nate thought it was a great idea, so he got down and gave one to Morgan too. I looked over at Morgan and smiled, "This is much better than rifle marksmanship."

By the time we were finished, Sam and Nate had their ankles linked while Morgan and I had our way with our respective boyfriends. I thought about playing with Nate's toes because he had some cute ones, but ultimately decided it best to preserve that little mystery for Sam and me.

11

The second half of our training was all about operating under combat situations. We bivouacked (used our small two-man tents in the field) for a week, did a thirteen-mile march and participated in an all-night live-fire exercise. If you can imagine crawling in the sand under strands of barbed wire while live rounds whiz overhead, you definitely have an idea of what it was like.

During the day, we conducted several important training exercises. NBC (Nuclear, Biological, and Chemical) training was one of the most crucial elements. We got to dress in our MOPP gear for several hours at a time. MOPP, for Mission Oriented Protected Posture, was Army speak for our heavy charcoal lined suits that offered protection against chemical agents. We also had to wear our gas masks and learn how to drink from our canteens through the little tube on our masks. We also learned how to administer atropine from the training injectors we were given. Atropine could help alleviate reactions to many chemical agents.

Sam knew that Troy and I had talked. He didn't mind if Troy and I were buddies as much as I didn't mind he was getting closer to Dane. We were secure in our relationship with each other.

Even though Troy and I were assigned as buddies, it didn't mean we did all our extra duties together. Dane and I had the pleasure of spending four hours together in a foxhole, on guard duty. At least it wasn't freezing cold outside. Since we were operating under light and noise discipline, we had to whisper back and forth. When Dane whispered, he got right in my ear. I could tell something was up with him by the way he was acting. Normally he was the outgoing type, but when we were in the foxhole together he seemed quiet and nervous.

When I couldn't take it any longer, I decided to do something about it. I leaned in close and whispered, "Is something on your mind, Dane?"

He didn't answer right away, but eventually leaned in and replied. "Is Sam seeing anyone back home?"

I didn't like the way he phrased it. If he had asked in the same manner Troy did, I would have been more forthcoming. He didn't spend much time around Troy, so I figured they might not have had a chance to talk about our earlier discussion. I answered in the safest way possible, "Dane, you should talk to Sam about this, not me."

"He told me he was seeing someone back home, but wouldn't give me any details."

Since I took Psychology, I tried a different tact. "Maybe it was the way you asked the question."

"I don't know what you mean."

I turned to face him and scooted in slightly closer. "Why do you think he would be hesitant to talk about it?"

Dane was quiet for a long time. I was hoping he would forget the whole discussion, because I wasn't going to out my boyfriend and get us kicked out before our careers even started. No such luck... "You are the one he's seeing back home, aren't you?"

I didn't confirm or deny, I just looked at him.

Moments later, Dane grinned. "Actually I think that's totally cool. I can see why the two of you are together."

"Are you not in a position to see someone when you are back home?"

Dane took a drink from his canteen. "Not really, I'm not sure how my family would react. I'm still living at home."

It wasn't my place, but I said it anyway. "Maybe you should complete your final year of college with Troy…"

"Holy shit…Really?"

I put my hand on his leg to calm him. "I'll say something to him if you'd like. It would be better if I prepared him before you say anything."

"I can't just up and move to Kansas. He barely even talks to me."

I had a better idea. "Yeah, but there's nothing preventing you from taking an extra day or two to go back home." Then I had the best idea of all, "Or I could talk him into visiting Colorado sometime during the summer. We still have a few weeks left."

"Oh my God, that would be so cool."

The final exercise we had to endure was a full-scale invasion of a fictitious town. We were issued paint guns and goggles to make it more realistic. Our training platoon was split into four separate squads; Troy and I got to be squad leaders for the evolution. Since there were others who were doing equally well, the instructors decided not to move any more people around. Sam was in a completely different squad and Dane was in the same one with me. Our squad's objective was to link with Troy's and move on the town from the south. The other two squads were going to attempt the same from the west.

The fictitious town was in the middle of the woods, so it wasn't going to be easy getting there. The squads responsible for the western portion also had a wide creek to deal with. We had our own hazards to contend with; the instructors promised an ambush somewhere in the forest. They were even nice enough to indicate the most probable locations where we would be attacked.

I knew they were full of shit.

We also got a military intelligence briefing just like it was the real deal. The intelligence briefers took great care in going over the potential ambush sites in even more detail.

Whatever… I knew how the instructors operated by then. I was fairly certain the ambush would take place in a completely different place. I felt comfortable reading the maps, but I would need to see the area with my own eyes before I knew for sure.

Topographic maps were pretty simple, the closer the little squiggly lines get together the higher the terrain. I knew there were several elevated areas in the way of our objective, but it was still difficult to figure out where a potential ambush would occur without being there.

When the hairs started to stand up on the back of my neck, I knew we were at the right place. There was a particularly dense grouping of trees ahead on an elevated slope about fifty yards ahead. The thicker stand of trees was long enough to hold an entire squad. I held my hand up to silently stop our squad. To my right, I could see a way through the forest. It was overgrown and looked like no one had been through there for years. Except I could see a few telltale bent blades of foliage and a couple of snapped twigs. Dad wouldn't have neglected to tell us how to track in the wild, after all. Just to be fair, we also had a brief class on it. I was glad I paid attention.

Trent Steele, who was in the role as the squad's senior sergeant came up beside me. I could tell he didn't agree with me. We'd shared a few heated words here and there during the past few weeks, but never anything nasty. "Why are we stopping?"

I pointed to the dense vegetation along the path we were taking. "If I was going to hide a squad to ambush ours, that's exactly where I would put it."

Trent didn't agree with me, as usual, and huffed to accentuate his displeasure with me. "I think we should follow the instructions we were given at the briefing and continue on the path. The real ambush site is two klicks ahead."

I nodded my head to show I was listening. I called for Troy on the radio and he approached moments later. He instantly agreed with my assessment.

Just to be sure, I took my field glasses and searched carefully for a clue. Any other time, I would have probably missed it, but I briefly saw the telltale sign of sunlight reflecting off another pair of field glasses in the distance, approximately at the three o'clock position from where we were standing, maybe a thousand yards in the distance. I handed them to Troy, "Three o'clock, a thousand yards out, tell me if you see anything."

Troy hitched in a breath a few seconds later. He handed the field glasses back to me, pulled me aside and whispered. "I think I saw our friendly lieutenant colonel out there observing us."

I nodded. "I've noticed he likes to stay clear of the action." I pointed to the area between the lieutenant colonel and where I thought the ambush squad was hidden. "We should go through there and attack from behind."

Troy nodded in agreement. "Let's do an l-shaped formation right down the middle to cut them off from this avenue of escape." He consulted his map further and pointed at a position on the other side of the dense stand of trees. "We can gather here to get ready for our assault on the town." He looked up and grinned at me. "The added advantage is we bypass all the suspected ambush points we were told about in the briefing. It should be smooth sailing from that point."

"I agree."

The ambush squad wasn't happy we figured out their game. As we got closer, they started to move. Since they no longer had the element of surprise and were facing the wrong way, we managed to get by with two casualties.

We took the town about an hour later.

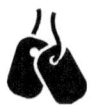

The day before we were scheduled to depart was a busy one. We were cleaning our equipment and getting everything checked in. Sam and I were side-by-side in the gymnasium where we were all assembled, giving our rifles a final thorough cleaning before inspection. Since we were good at passing inspections, we had several others working beside us. They wanted us to check their weapons before handing them in to the instructors.

The head instructor came into the room and I could tell he was heading straight for us. Sam and I, along with the others, jumped to attention. The instructor was his usual gruff self, "Cadet Carter and Cadet Rogers, grab your weapons and come with me."

It was no big deal since our rifles were fully assembled. We followed along to an office that was down a long hallway. Our instructor knocked on the door and opened it after hearing a loud, "Enter!"

Sam and I were faced with the grey haired lieutenant colonel who had been watching us all month. He was standing when we entered the room. "Cadets, please take a seat." He looked to our instructor and nodded.

When we were alone, the lieutenant colonel reached for my weapon, "Your rifle, if you please."

Apparently his observations weren't finished. I was confident that he would find a perfectly cleaned and operational weapon. The colonel stripped my weapon down in a matter of seconds and carefully checked every square inch with a flash light. When he was done, he pushed the disassembled parts to my side of the table. "You may take a seat and reassemble your weapon." Then he gave Sam's weapon the same treatment.

The colonel didn't say anything about the cleanliness of our weapons, instead he took a seat after Sam had his rifle back together. "I'll give you one guess who I work for."

Sam and I didn't need even one. At the same time, we said, "Special Forces."

He smiled and offered his hand to each of us. "Gentlemen, I am Lieutenant Colonel Ford Cooper and it is my job to recruit officers for the Special Forces. I have been observing you and the other cadets during training." He looked at each of us carefully. "Any guess as to why I asked to speak to you?"

I had a pretty good idea. "Are you here to persuade us not to be engineers?"

Colonel Cooper chuckled in response. "Gentlemen, training in Special Forces is by invitation only. It will be the hardest thing you have ever done. You are looking at a training program that can last for two years. At the end, you will officially be eighteen-alphas, or Special Forces officers." He let his words sink in before he continued. "I feel the two of you have potential to be outstanding combat leaders. If you are interested in training with us, you will need to be captains with a successful combat command under your belts. I think you should think seriously about becoming infantry officers. It will give you what you need to succeed." He stopped and stared the two of us down. "I have your names and you can be assured I will be contacting you the moment you become eligible."

Sam and I both agreed to his idea at the same time and Sam spoke for both of us. "Sir, your plan sounds like a good one, that's what we'll do."

Colonel Cooper nodded his head. "Excellent, you are dismissed. Do me a favor and have Cadets Cooper and Atherton report to me."

I stood up and took a big risk. The colonel and I weren't buddies, but I had to know. "Sir, by any chance do you know my dad?"

Colonel Cooper nodded one time. "You bet your ass I do. I'll be calling him in a couple of hours." Before we left the room, he had one more bit of advice. "Gentlemen, use your last year of college wisely. I would recommend taking Arabic language classes if your school offers them. It will help you get through Special Forces training that much quicker if you are already proficient, as that part of the world also has the highest deployment potential for the members of our command. You should also practice your breast stroke while wearing your uniforms. You'll need to be able to swim at least fifty meters, fully dressed, to qualify for entrance to our training program."

Sam and I felt great about our decision. I wish we would have known it would have such a huge impact on our lives.

Summer 2000

To say my dad was excited to see us at the airport would have been the understatement of the year. He hugged Sam and me both when we came off the jetway. "I am extremely proud of both of you."

We were pretty happy ourselves. I decided to give Dad a hard time. "Did you enjoy your daily reports from Colonel Cooper?"

"More like weekly, but the last one was the best of all." Dad frowned for a moment. "I have no idea how I'm going to tell your mother about this. She's not going to be nearly as excited as I am."

I knew what to do. "We'll tell her together."

Dad talked a mile-a-minute the entire way to baggage claim. "Colonel Cooper told me he had a productive month. He said he took four names as potential candidates for Special Forces training, do you know the other two?"

Sam laughed. "Actually, they were our buddies the whole time."

"Good, you should invite them to visit before the summer is over. I'd like to meet them."

I was happy to hear that. "I'll get it taken care of."

Dane and Troy arrived about two weeks later. Dane flew in from Oregon and Troy drove from Kansas; he had an old mint-green 1967 Chevrolet pickup truck. The color wasn't the only thing about it that was mint—Troy was good at working on cars. When he got to our house, he spent forty-five minutes checking out our Cherokee. I could tell he was dying to get his hands on it.

Mom was still pretty sore with me. And Sam... And Dad... In her opinion, it was bad enough we wanted to be in Special Forces, but having to serve in the Infantry to be eligible was almost more than she could bear. At least she was talking to us. The first week had been very chilly. Her attitude softened noticeably when she met Troy and Dane. She liked them a lot and felt better about Sam and me serving with guys like them. It already looked like the four of us were going to be able to do most of our training together. She interrogated them thoroughly and decided they were all right after they answered her questions satisfactorily.

Sam's parents were pissed at him too. He needed a break from his folks and their constant arguing about our career choice, so when Troy and Dane arrived he stayed at the house with the rest of us.

Sam and I enjoyed every bit of it, it was the first time we had slept together in one of our actual bedrooms. It was nice to have experiences with him in real time. My twin bed was kind of small for the both of us, so we spent our nights on the floor in our sleeping bags, which we promptly zipped together so we could share.

Morgan and Nate joined in on the fun on their side of the room. We had definitely gotten past the point of being shy when it came to having sex with our boyfriends in front of each other. Morgan insisted on a nightly jerk-off contest since we were all together, Troy and Dane were more than happy to participate.

Dane and Troy got the biggest kick out of my dad. They weren't intimidated by him in the least, and they had a lot of fun sitting with him on the patio and drinking beer. Sam and I stuck to iced-tea, neither of us cared much for beer yet.

Even though we had a lot of work to do in the shop, Dad let us have some free time together. Dane and Troy didn't have a problem pitching in each morning so we could hang out the rest of the day.

On the second day of their visit, Troy and I got a little extra time together because Dad sent us to the lumber yard for more supplies. I was stoked to get some alone time with him and another opportunity to drive my dad's truck. I was eager to hear how Troy and Dane were getting along. I had seen them give each other multiple blowjobs the night before. I was curious if they liked each other. Once we were on our way, I asked him about it. "How are things with you and Dane?"

Troy let loose with his happy laugh. "Man, it has been so nice to be able to play with a dick that isn't mine."

"Is this going to be a one-time thing or have you talked about seeing more of each other?"

Troy was quiet for a minute or two. "I don't think we're going to be each other's forever guy."

"That's sad to hear, you two look good together."

Troy didn't appear too sad about it. "We've definitely had some fun, but he's clearly attracted to someone else."

"Sam?" The thought made sense, they spent a lot of time around each other at Fort Lewis.

Troy's answer surprised me. "Actually he really likes your brother."

Troy and I were becoming good friends. Sam and I were solid, but for some reason I felt it was important for Troy to know what I was thinking. "If Sam and I weren't together, I would've been the one sucking your dick last night."

"Oh my God, really?" He shook his head and smiled, "Believe me, I feel the same." He was quiet for a moment and softly added, "I'm glad we can be friends though."

When we got back, Morgan had the rest of the day planned. Once Dad was out of earshot, he filled us in. He had a crucial question to ask Troy and Dane, "Did you guys bring swimsuits?"

They shook their heads in unison.

Morgan's huge smile indicated he was happy with the development. That was alarming to me because I only knew of one place where we could do such a thing. I couldn't imagine he would take us to the pond or the pool on the mansion's grounds. Jason had made it very clear from the beginning that his invitation to the house was only for the four of us.

Morgan directed his attention to Troy and Dane. "We have a special place for swimming we would like to show you. It's nice and private. We like to go there all the time."

I stared daggers at my brother, and tried valiantly to shoot him with my psychic death-ray.

Morgan ignored me and went for the cooler he already packed. Sam picked up a stack of beach towels, he shrugged at me as we walked out of the shop together, he had no idea what my brother was up to either.

Since Morgan was in charge, he drove the Jeep. I was in the back seat with Sam, Troy, and Dane, while Nate was up front. It was a tight fit, but not that big of a deal since we were all buddies, and Sam was seated on my lap.

Morgan chatted happily about our favorite swimming spot the entire way. I felt a tightness in my chest as he took the highway towards Estes Park, the same road that lead to the Buchanan Mansion. Sam squeezed my leg because he could sense my unease.

I felt a huge sense of relief when Morgan continued down the road past the house. He finally pulled into a driveway about four miles down the road from the mansion. We drove past a large red barn on our way to a pond that turned out to be much nicer than the one at the Buchanan property. It was nicely shielded by a grove of pine and aspen. There was a huge oak tree with a rope swing that jutted out over the pond. Instead of a dock, this pond had a smooth-pebbled beach.

When Morgan stopped, we got out of the Jeep and the others started to unload the cooler, the towels, and our camp chairs. Since the others were busy, I took my brother by the arm and hauled him a discreet distance away. "Why have you never told me about this place?"

Morgan pulled his arm from my grasp and gave my shoulder a hard push. "Chill! Nate and I discovered it a couple of weeks ago." He grinned, "We don't spend every spare minute at the mansion, we do like to get out and explore." He gave me a glare, "You and Sam ought to try it sometime."

Because I have always been the more responsible of the two of us, I expressed my concern. "Do you have permission to be here?"

Morgan's eyes flashed with irritation, but he eventually broke into a mischievous grin, "Yes, Dad."

I was still in *Dad Mode*, "Explain."

Morgan huffed dramatically. "You're going to be one of those asshole officers aren't you?" He continued before I could give a proper retort. "Remember that big cabinet order we were finishing up when you and Sam left for Fort Lewis? This land belongs to the client. We got to talking about swimming and he told us we were more than welcome to come here."

I smiled at my brother indulgently, "Okay, I wanted to make sure." Then I gave him a wink, "You have a tendency to jump into things without thinking them all the way through."

We had a breaststroke competition, which Troy beat all of us in—repeatedly. We acted like kids when it came to the rope swing. It was a nice time. When we got tired of swimming, we put our boxers on and set up our camp chairs. Morgan packed a light lunch for all of us, and we got to answer a million questions from Morgan and Nate about our month in Washington. Sam and I had Cokes while the others drank a few beers, it was a perfect day.

Sam ended up in my lap with his legs hanging over the side of our chair. It was so nice to be able to be open with him again. I kissed him on the temple. "We should've brought our BDU's to see how far we can swim in them." I was mainly joking, but we needed to start thinking about our military future.

Sam surprised me when he jumped out of my lap and went to the Jeep. When he came back, he was carrying our uniforms and combat boots.

I groaned.

Dane got up and ran around to the rear of the Jeep and came back with two more sets for him and Troy. He looked at me and laughed, "No time like the present."

The four of us got out of our boxers because we wanted to keep them dry and started getting dressed. Morgan and Nate pulled off their boxers and joined us in the water. They swam approximately fifty meters and hovered, so we would know where to stop.

Fifty meters doesn't sound that far, but when weighed down by heavy combat boots and a uniform, it's a long haul. Thankfully we didn't have to wear a fully loaded pack too. Fortunately, the pond was only about five feet deep, so we weren't going to drown. The four of us made it in good time and floated around on our backs until we had the energy to swim back. I was thankful for all the PT that Dad put us through. We wouldn't have been able to do it if he hadn't.

We had to check out the barn before we went home. There was a very important reason, because barns tended to have haylofts and haylofts were a good place to have fun. We were in our shorts and flip-flops, but decided to remain shirtless.

The loft was half full of hay bales and the floor had a thick layer scattered all over it. I watched Morgan as he spread out the towels he brought with him. My little brother was up to no good.

Since I had always thoroughly enjoyed calling him out on things whenever possible, I did so again. I stared him down, which never had any affect, and crossed my arms over my chest.

Morgan looked at me and started laughing. Then he turned his attention to Troy and Dane. "You two have had some fun with each other since you've been here. I think you need some experience with a different dick or two before you leave." He carefully surveyed the rest of us. "I think it might be a good idea for the rest of us too."

I started to pace. While his idea had merit, I felt bad because the only other dick in the barn I truly wanted to suck was Troy's. Sam and I had never been with anyone else. I wasn't sure I wanted him to know I liked Troy that much. My brother had done an excellent job of getting me into a sticky situation.

Sam pulled me to the side. "You have my permission, as long as I get to watch."

"Are you sure?"

Sam squeezed my ass and nodded. "Max, I love you. Morgan's right though, we should do this because at some point, we are going to start wondering about it. I would feel more comfortable if we did this with people we trust."

Morgan came up to my other side and squeezed my ass too. "Don't worry, it's only a blowjob, that's practically a handshake among gay guys."

I agreed with him, but I still gave him a good hard shove. I laughed when he almost fell on his ass, but then frowned, "It's going to be such a happy day when I knock you on your ass."

Morgan stuck his tongue out at me. "Good luck with that, I work out just as much as you do."

The others were laughing and having a good time, so I relaxed. It seemed like they wanted to indulge Morgan, so I decided it wasn't that bad of an idea since Sam was with me.

We kicked off our flip-flops and took off our shorts. Troy walked towards me. I figured Sam would go to Dane, but he surprised me—and Morgan—by going to Nate and getting on his knees in front of him. Troy told me to lay down and he got comfortable in between my legs.

We had a good time. It was actually super-hot to see Sam giving Nate a blowjob. Troy gave me an excellent one and Morgan had Dane on top of him in a sixty-nine.

I watched Nate return the favor to Sam as I had Troy get on top of me and pump into my mouth. It wasn't Sam, but it was nice. Troy was a lot bigger than Sam or me.

By the time we were finished, we basically had a buffet going on—with the exception of me and my brother. I was relieved when it came time to blow my boyfriend, because we had been saving our load for each other. When we were done, we headed home for dinner.

After we grilled steaks on the patio, Mom and Dad decided to go for a walk. The rest of us stayed on the patio, enjoying each other's company. Like usual, Sam was in my lap with his legs hanging over the arm of the chair. Morgan and Nate were situated similarly. Dane and Troy were sitting close at the picnic table.

We were very surprised when the back gate opened and Sam's mom and dad came into the yard. What a way to come out! They were basically speechless, but managed to tell Sam that he needed to get his ass home pronto.

My heart beat faster when Sam told his parents we had been in love since they moved to Boulder.

I felt the same way, but I kept the true timeline to myself, I had been in love with him for months before we even met.

13

Early Military Service 2001-2003

Sam and I graduated college in 2001. Morgan and Nate had another year before they got their nerd degrees in computer science. Too bad I can't call him a nerd to his face because he'd put me on my ass in a hurry. He's a big guy.

Sam's parents took a while to come around. Much of their acceptance of our relationship was a result of spending more time with my parents—and Nate's.

There was also a little bit of supernatural intervention, which we learned about shortly before we shipped out to Fort Benning for our seventeen weeks of infantry officer training.

Sam's parents made a big effort in trying to understand our relationship. Because of that, they started spending more time at the house and having dinner with my family and Nate's. One evening, Sam's mom seemed especially upset and she started crying.

Since my mom was a psychiatrist, she asked Sam's mom if she would like to talk about it.

Sam's mom pulled a Kleenex from her purse and dabbed at her eyes. "I met the nicest young man in our office today. He's seventeen years old and he came in asking for a quote for an automobile policy. I told him I would need to speak to his parents because he was under eighteen. He pulled out the paperwork from the court proclaiming his emancipation." Her tears started to flow again, "I know it wasn't any of my business, but I had to ask why he was an emancipated minor."

She broke into sobs and Sam's dad took over for her. "This perfectly adjusted, good-looking boy told us how his parents kicked him out of the house when they found out he was gay. He had no one in his family who was willing to take him in, so he petitioned the court and was declared an adult. He has a full-time job waiting tables and is starting college in the fall." Sam's dad shook his head. "He is an amazing young-man with a lot of promise."

Sam's mother regained her composure enough to take over again. "It really got both of us to thinking." She looked at Sam and me. "You two have loved each other since you met. I just want you to know we love both of you and are very proud of the men you have become." She sniffled some more, "I am sorry that it has taken us so long to come around."

It was the best dinner ever. There were a lot of hugs.

Morgan the interrogator, wanted details. "Do you remember his name? I know about scholarships and youth groups he might not be familiar with. I'd like to help him out if I could."

Sam's mom smiled at my brother. "You're such a sweetie, Morgan. His name was Tyler Ridgeway."

Morgan and I exchanged a quick glance; we both began to wonder if she was describing some more of Jason's meddling. It helped explain why we didn't see him very often. He was obviously much busier than we originally thought.

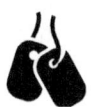

Sam and I were split up after infantry training. Sam and Dane got their first commands as platoon leaders for the First Infantry Division in Fort Riley, Kansas. I missed Sam, but I got to see him whenever I wanted.

I got to serve with Troy, so at least there was a friendly face with me at our first duty station in the Republic of Korea, as platoon leaders in the 8th US Army.

South Korea was an excellent place to learn how to lead troops in a wartime setting. There was an armistice in place since 1953 that halted the Korean conflict, but the two sides were still technically at war because they never signed a peace agreement. For the first time we got to see what it was like to be in a situation where war could erupt at any second, Troy and I learned very quickly to have ourselves squared away at all times.

My relationship with Sam didn't suffer too much from being so far away. Our link with the Buchanan Mansion worked without a problem. When Sam and I were in Fort Benning, we decided to try a little experiment; he wanted to see what it looked like when one of us jumped to the mansion. Since closets were no longer involved, we had taken to using Jason's original term of *jumping*. We bunked next to each other and were curious if the jumping process was noticeable to anyone else. That worry was always at the back of our minds and it kept us from going as much as we wanted in those early days. After I jumped, and returned moments later, Sam had a big smile on his face. He said he didn't notice a thing.

On average, we jumped to the mansion three to four times a week. Sometimes we would stay for an hour or two, other times, we stayed for a couple of days. Army life was hard work and it was nice to have some downtime with each other. We also used the opportunity to do a lot of swimming so we would be ready for the fifty-meter challenge when we tried out for Special Forces.

Mom and Dad came to South Korea to visit once Troy and I saved up a few days of leave, it was nice to see them, but the visit was a little tense on the last day when Dad took me aside and asked if Troy and I were together. I told him we weren't, but it didn't seem like Dad believed me. I didn't like how he had written off my relationship with

Sam, but there wasn't a good way for me to tell him I saw Sam all the time.

The four of us were promoted to First Lieutenant within days of each other, around the time we had been on active duty for eighteen months. Once we hit our two years, we were moved again.

Sam and Dane became platoon leaders at different companies in the First Infantry Division, they also got deployed to Iraq together.

Troy and I got to stay together; we were assigned to the 22nd Infantry Regiment and were deployed to the mountains of Afghanistan to root out insurgents. We operated out of a fire base not far from the mountains, spending most of our time in search of the enemy and the rest defending our base. Troy and I remained platoon leaders like Sam and Dane.

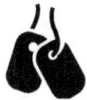

Once the four of us were deployed in actual combat, my visits with Sam began to slowly taper off. We had proven beyond the shadow of a doubt no one could tell when we left, but it didn't seem right when those we served with couldn't do the same. At one point, Sam and I only saw each other about once a month.

All four of us had seen some bad things. Sam and Dane witnessed the horrible after effects of an IED explosion in northern Iraq after they were in-country a few weeks. Sam lost three members of his platoon from the explosion and I could tell it changed him. He had to spend a week in the hospital because of a constant ringing in his ears. The day before he was scheduled to be sent to Germany, and possibly discharged, the ringing abruptly stopped.

Troy and I had a bad experience while on patrol in Afghanistan. We had to achieve a careful balance of adequate space between each other in the event of an explosion, and not getting so far apart that we were combat ineffective. We heard the explosion about a hundred yards in front of us. Once the area was deemed clear, we came upon Private Wilkinson. What we saw was even more chilling than what you would imagine a scene like that to be. Private Wilkinson didn't have a scratch on him, but he was clearly dead. Our medic told us he most likely died from the shock wave.

We usually managed some downtime after two or three weeks of constant patrol. Our firebase was by no means luxurious, but it was heaven compared to a winding path, swarming with insurgents who wanted to kill us. We didn't use tents on the firebase because we needed fortified shelters able to withstand mortar attacks. Troy and I shared quarters.

Towards the end of our time there, my friendship with Troy changed dramatically. We had just returned from our last mission and we were both desperate to take a shower. I told Troy to go first because I was a little on the horny side and I needed some time alone. I thought it would be nice for Troy to have the same when he got back.

I was worried while I took my shower, being around Troy all the time was starting to weigh on me because I truly enjoyed his company. It was to the point where the only two people I knew better were Morgan and Sam. My resolve was starting to wear down. Thankfully, he was the only one who gave me those thoughts. There was another platoon leader Troy and I served with who was sort of cute, but his frequent quoting of biblical scripture kept my interest right where it should be. I had half a mind to jump to the mansion and demand Jason tell Sam to meet me.

Not that it would work, we still only saw him at Christmas.

I took an extra-long shower because I had two weeks' worth of grime to rinse off. I got dressed in a clean uniform and made my way back to our quarters. I had been gone for a half hour, so I reasoned it should have been plenty of time.

It wasn't.

I was in full-on gape mode when I opened the door, Troy was in the midst of rubbing one out and it was one of the hottest things I'd seen in months. I'd sucked Troy's dick one time and it was still at the top of my hottest encounters. I felt guilty as hell for using it as masturbation material, but it was always guaranteed to get the job done—and quickly.

Troy was irritated with me, but not for interrupting him. "Close the fucking door, Lieutenant."

I smiled sheepishly and did as he asked. "Sorry, my mind sort of blanked out…"

He was half-lidded and sexy as he continued to stroke himself. "See something you like?"

I nodded slowly.

"Don't you think it's about time you did something about it?"

My eyes grew big. Reality was beginning to set in. "I want to, but I shouldn't."

Troy's reply was reasonable. "You haven't seen Sam for ages and it's going to be several more months before you do. I think we could at least suck each other off. What's the harm in that?"

I could've argued with him, but there was no way I could tell him the truth. Even though Sam and I weren't jumping as much. I guess I decided it would be easier to do what we both wanted than to make him think I was crazy. I probably could've made him think I was a saint by refusing to cheat on Sam, but somehow I knew he would be able to tell I was full of shit.

I got naked like my clothes were on fire. I gave silent thanks to whoever came up with the idea for quick release laces on our combat boots. I took my place in the void between his spread legs. I didn't do anything right away because I was mesmerized just looking at his dick. He had a big one, nice and thick with perfect porn-star proportions. I'd seen and tasted it before, but I didn't verbalize how pretty it was. It would have been extremely rude to say something like that in front of Sam. I ran my finger along the inside curve from base to tip and gave the thick head a squeeze.

Troy gurgled his approval and bucked his hips upward to maintain contact with my hand.

I chuckled and traced my finger down the front of his cock and gave his balls a slight tug. Troy was thicker than the rest of us by far. With Sam, Nate, myself (and Morgan by default, because we were the same), I could make a ring out of my thumb and forefinger that just managed to go all the way around. I wasn't able to do the same with Troy. I had to know, so I tried. There was about an eighth-of-an-inch gap between my thumb and forefinger. I sat there for a moment looking at it, I wanted it in my ass because it had been months since I had Sam inside of me.

I felt like the most horrible person on earth for having such a thought.

Troy pulled his feet up and rested them against my knees. He knew what I was thinking, but his expression remained playful. "You like my big dick don't you?"

I nodded truthfully.

Troy went from satisfied to concerned, "We don't have to do anything you feel uncomfortable with." He reached out and started playing with my dick. "I can tell you need to let some steam off though. It's been a long time for both of us."

I'm sure it had been much longer for him. Troy was my friend and it was safe to say he was my best friend. Surely messing around with him wouldn't be a mortal sin. Getting naked with him and being a cock-tease certainly wasn't friendly. Instead of saying anything, I bent down and took his big porn star dick in my mouth.

Blowing him was heavenly, he was so long and thick. He was very squirmy, which was cute as hell. I spent several minutes torturing him with my tongue and by swallowing around him. He got a little rambunctious with the process by grabbing both sides of my head and thrusting upward, I let him have his fun because I enjoyed it too.

When he got close, he pushed me off and gave me some torment of his own.

When I got close, he seemed to sense it and pulled off. He sat up and scooted in closer. "Did you like that?"

I nodded. "I need to come in the worst way."

Troy smiled and leaned in. Before he did anything, he stopped. "If this is too much, tell me to stop."

I answered by pulling him in and kissing him.

Troy broke the kiss after a few minutes and leaned backwards on his hands. "Have you given any thought about how you would like to come?"

I'd done nothing but think about it, but I still wasn't quite sure if it was a good idea. I wrinkled my forehead. "Maybe we should give each other a nice hand job."

"Is that what you really want?"

I was embarrassed with how meek my answer was. "No…"

Troy grinned and reached for my dick. "Would you like to fuck me?"

Troy and I talked about a lot, but we didn't talk much about my sex life with Sam. He had no way of knowing what I preferred when it came to *that*. I slowly shook my head.

His look was priceless—surprise, disbelief, maybe amazement. "Really?"

"I don't think you have to be that dramatic…"

Troy put his hand on my forehead. "I need to make sure you aren't running a fever."

I grabbed him by the wrist, "Ha-ha. I like to be on the bottom most of the time." Pretty much all of the time, but I wasn't ready to tell him everything.

"But you're such a big guy…"

I gave his dick a nice stroke. "So are you…"

To make a long story short, our first time together—in the biblical sense—was intense. I had my hands on Troy's ass the entire time. We laughed and kissed each other senseless. He fucked me like I'd never been fucked before.

It was a little too good.

Fall 2003

The four of us had new orders, assigned as a group to Fort Carson, Colorado as part of the 4th Infantry Division. None of us would be serving together, but we would be on the same post. We got to move up the chain a little bit as executive officers at our respective companies. The Army wanted us to have more company-level experience before beginning our Special Forces training. It was a good place to park us until we became captains and we would be busy training replacements for the ongoing wars in Iraq and Afghanistan.

The four of us met in Germany at Ramstein for the flight home. For the duration of my trip, I had to play it cool and not do any of the traditional things lovers do when they hadn't seen each other for months.

Sam and I hadn't seen each other for three months and only once in the two-month period before that. When I saw the prominent scar on his cheek, I understood why. I tried to hold it back, but I started crying.

It was a difficult trip. I already felt like I lived in an alternate universe with the Buchanan Mansion. Now I felt like I was part of another, where I couldn't show my concern for the man I loved.

It was a tense flight home and the discomfort of it made things worse. We were in a C-17 configured for passengers, so it was noisy and we were crammed together like sardines. We shared a few tense words on the flight back, I was pissed off at him for not telling me what happened to him.

I did the best I could to keep my emotions in check. I blinked furiously to keep the tears at bay. Sam discreetly put his hand next to mine and gave it a squeeze. That simple gesture made things so much better between the two of us. I was in peace for the rest of the flight.

We had a few days leave before we had to report to Fort Carson. Troy and Dane spent the night with us before they left for some downtime in Kansas and Oregon respectively. Sam's parents were glad to see him, so he decided to stay with them while in town. We were going to have plenty of time together. We needed to get back in the game where our workouts were concerned. Not a lot of chances to go running and swimming in the mountains of Afghanistan or the deserts of Iraq.

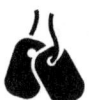

About a week after we arrived at Fort Carson, I had a dream. Instead of Sam, Morgan came to me in my sleep. He was as irritating in my dream as real life, he kept repeating the same message over and over. "I need you at the mansion."

I was tired and would have preferred for him to shut the hell up, but I knew my brother well. He would keep at it until I relented. I decided to do as he asked, because none of us had ever been able to speak to each other in our dreams before.

I mouthed the magic word and found myself on the terrace with my brother. It was a picture perfect hot, sunny day. I appreciated it because it was really the middle of November. Morgan sat in his swim suit in one of the lounge chairs with a beer.

I greeted him in my usual smart-ass way. "I'm fairly sure you aren't dead, so I'm assuming the house has given us a new power?"

Morgan hopped out of the lounger and gave me an enthusiastic hug. "Jason told me to try it out. He wanted to see if it worked." Then he snapped his fingers and a Coca Cola appeared in his hand. "Here, this is for you."

I noticed he didn't seem his usual happy self. "Morgan, is something wrong?"

He took a seat. "I need to talk to you about some stuff."

I joined him in the same lounger, it was way too small for both of us, but it was fun to be a pain in the ass. Morgan looked me over critically. I was in my uniform pants and t-shirt. "Were you on duty?"

"No, this was the only thing I had handy to put on. I was in bed." I yawned dramatically to make my point.

Morgan took a long draw off his beer. He was silent for several moments. "Mom and Dad have decided to do some traveling. Mom quit the hospital, her last day at work is next Friday."

This wasn't a huge shock because they had been talking about it since we were in high school. They were set as far as money was concerned and the house was paid for; Mom made good money as an ER Psychiatrist, and Dad substantially added to their savings with his cabinet business. I congratulated myself for being such a stellar son and having my college education completely paid for, so they wouldn't have to worry about that. Morgan's education was similarly taken care of because of his scholarship and his huge brain.

"What are they going to do with the house?" I braced myself for the reply. Morgan had been making statements here and there over the past year about me coming home for good.

"They are keeping the house and I'm going to keep an eye on it for them." Morgan stared me down hard for two long minutes before he continued. "Dad is saving all his tools for you."

Yeah, the Squirt really wanted me home. Instead of getting into an old issue, I squeezed his knee; hard enough to make him squirm.

It's a big brother's job to make the little one squirm as much as possible. "Is Nate moving in with you?"

"Nate is in San Francisco."

Morgan's news caught me off guard. "What do you mean? How long is he going to be there?"

Morgan was in the mood for another beer, so I followed him in the house. He could have snapped his fingers for another one, but he chose to go inside. I was certain he was purposely wasting time. Once we were in the kitchen and Morgan had his beer, he continued. "Nate took a job at Google. He's tired of Colorado and wants to be in California." Morgan rolled his eyes like it was the dumbest thing he had ever heard, "Not much I can do about it. He's been talking about it since we met."

I was dumbfounded. Were all our relationships hitting a rough patch at the same time? I was going to be in a lot of trouble when I told my brother about the state of things with Sam. A lot like the trouble he was in with me for doing the same. "How long?"

"Three months."

My nostrils flared. "And you're just getting around to telling me?" I shook my head, "Nice…"

Morgan knew exactly what to say. "I talked to Sam a few days ago."

"Nope, we're not going to talk about me and Sam, we are still discussing you and Nate."

Morgan assured me our discussion about Nate was over. "Don't you dare give me any shit for not telling you Nate moved away. Sam told me he didn't see you for three months before you got assigned to Fort Carson." Morgan took a long drink. "Oh, and let's not forget that you and Troy are fucking."

I was instantly reminded of an unpleasant conversation with Sam. He wasn't pissed because he'd done the same thing with Dane, so I didn't feel horribly guilty, but there was still a divide between us— enough that he had to tell Morgan about it.

Morgan looked over at me, his eyes were tearing up. "Max, please come home. I can't take any more of this shit, I don't want to be alone. Resign your commission, come back here and we can build cabinets together." Morgan looked at me hopefully, "You and Sam can sort things out and we can hire a hottie to help us." He choked up, "It worked for you and Sam."

"Are you and Nate finished? Why can't he visit you here? I have to admit, it hasn't worked the best for me and Sam since we've been deployed, but we're still together." I had a few tears of my own to share, "Going into the Special Forces has been our dream for a long time. If I don't go with him, we'll be finished."

Morgan started crying, so I took him in my arms. I missed hugging my brother. I felt bad for seeing him even less than Sam. "Nate and I haven't spent much time here for the past year. This house and everything it represents has always been too much for him. He wants to have a normal life." Morgan cried even harder. "We're not seeing each other anymore."

I squeezed him extra hard. "Squirt, I promise I'll talk to Sam about it. Who knows, maybe he'll surprise me. I will make you a promise though, if I don't make it through the training, I'll quit the Army and come back here."

Morgan smiled for the first time. "Thanks, that's better than nothing." His expression became slightly demonic. He punched me in the shoulder and it wasn't a gentle one either. "Stop calling me Squirt!"

I made sure to promise Morgan that I would make more time for him before I left. I didn't want him to be alone. He was my little brother and we had to stick together.

Special Forces Training 2004-2006

Once we had our time in grade as First Lieutenants, the four of us got our Captains bars. We received our orders the same day to report for training at the John F. Kennedy Special Warfare Center and School at Fort Bragg, North Carolina.

The first stage of our training was the most terrifying; we had to go to airborne school. The first item on the menu was the static line jump, which took up our first three weeks.

I'd always considered myself to be pretty brave. I don't think I would have been as successful in the Army if I wasn't, but I didn't enjoy scary rides at the amusement park either. I tended to stay away from anything that went upside down or dropped after being hoisted up in the air. Morgan was always much braver than me when it came to that sort of thing. After all, he's the idiot who wanted to jump off a roof when we were kids.

After our airborne training, we quickly cycled through classes where we learned how to operate every conceivable weapon and vehicle in the Army's possession. We even learned the basics of operating a tank. We learned how to operate a wide array of nontraditional vehicles as well. We learned defensive driving in a beat-up Ford Crown Victoria and a couple of Chevy Impalas, as well as a variety of SUVs. Some were armored and others weren't. We needed to know how to handle the varying weight characteristics of both.

We learned how to shoot rifles and handguns accurately with both hands. Somewhere along the way, we figured we must have shot at least twenty-thousand rounds a month.

We also had to learn how to do each job in the squads we would be leading. By the time we were finished we were medics, weapons sergeants, communication specialists, and snipers; as well as leaders of a Special Forces operations detachment.

There were months of language training to endure as well. Since Sam and Dane had spent most of their time in Iraq, they already knew Arabic pretty well. By the time we were finished, they were practically dreaming in it. The same went for Troy and me, but our language was Pashto because that was what most people spoke in Afghanistan.

We learned how to storm a building using what many refer to as *The Conga Line*. We would line up at a door and each of us would focus our fire on a specific range of the compass. There was a lot of bobbing and weaving, so that's how the maneuver got its name. We trained on those tactics for months because they were the most important. We had to know how to make the split-second decision to shoot terrorists and spare the innocent.

We spent months learning survival training. Since Special Forces soldiers were trained to operate without backup, we had to learn how to forage for food and avoid anything poisonous. We learned how to build shelters, make fire from practically nothing, sanitize water, and dress an animal carcass.

We went through extensive training on how to track animals, and people, in the wild.

By the time our training was over, we were able to kill a human or an animal with just about anything—including our bare hands.

Since we passed the airborne portion of our training with little trouble, the Army saved the scarier stuff for later. Next up on the menu was HALO (High Altitude Low Opening) and HAHO (High Altitude High Opening) parachute training. In comparison, the static-line jumps we mastered earlier in the course didn't seem that bad. We took practice jumps from a variety of heights, usually around fifteen hundred feet or less. The high altitude jumps were a completely different ball game, we jumped at altitudes around 35,000 feet. The HALO jumps were easier because we weren't in the air as long. That's where the low-opening came into play; we would jump from a great height, drop like a rock and deploy our parachute at the last possible moment.

We used the Ram-Air Parachute System (RAPS) for our high-altitude jumps. This allowed us the ability to do what was called a stand-off drop. Stand-off drops were the most clandestine way to get into an area. Sometimes, the airplane we were jumping from didn't have to enter enemy airspace using this method. We could use our RAPS to glide in horizontally over long distances before descending vertically.

The training was by far the most difficult we had ever gone through, but we did it. The four of us wished we could have started with Special Forces and bypassed the regular Army. We were warriors and psyched to let the enemy know we were ready to bring some serious hurt.

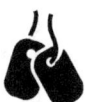

Morgan was having a better time of it during our training too. The Squirt got himself a new job with a consulting company that required frequent travel. He was involved with a big project with Facebook, which started to get really big. Morgan spent a lot of time in the Bay Area, but he didn't see Nate Conway at all.

My relationship with Sam wasn't perfect. We spent more time at the mansion, but a lot of it was at the pool. Sex with him was different. We still had it now and then, but not like our early days. He was much more gun-shy; kissing, rubbing, and blowjobs were still on the menu, but they seemed different. He wasn't into being carried around and he wasn't as sweet or funny.

We hadn't fucked for months.

I had a theory about what was going on in that cute head of his, and it wasn't something that would result in a happy conversation if I brought it up. I was pretty sure he wanted more space in the event something happened to one of us. The scar on his cheek was a daily reminder of the danger in our chosen profession.

During the last few weeks of training, Sam mentioned we should spend some time at the mansion. I was hopeful that he was starting to come around.

I decided to do something special for him. Army food wasn't that great, so I thought a nice dinner would be just the ticket for him. Sam liked to eat and fixing a dinner at the mansion was about as stress free as you could get.

After I had everything figured out, I gave Sam a cryptic message via our link to meet me at the mansion thirty minutes later. I knew he shared the ability to communicate like I did with Morgan, but we had yet to use it. I thought it would add a little intrigue to the situation.

I jumped to the house first, took a wonderful hot shower and put on my favorite Adidas track pants with the orange stripes and a clean white t-shirt. I figured dressing that way would be nice and low-key. I wanted our time together to be relaxing. I wanted to have sex with him, but I wanted to talk even more.

I had plans for a roasted turkey breast with his two favorite sides: garlic mashed potatoes and garden fresh green beans. I also had a chilled bottle of wine ready to go.

Whenever any of us jumped to the house, we automatically appeared in the room where the other was. Since I was in the kitchen, that's where Sam met me.

Sam smiled when he appeared in front of me. I smiled back, even though he promptly took my Coke and finished it. "Damn that was good."

I kissed him on the cheek. "Do you want some more?"

Sam shook his head. "I'm good. You're all nice and clean, I'm going to run upstairs and take a shower."

He needed to, but I wasn't going to tell him. I totally would have made out with him all sweaty and dirty, but I reminded myself that

Sam Rogers and I were going to do some talking first, over a nice meal.

Sam seemed happier than I'd seen him in a long time when he came back to the dining room. His eyes practically glazed over at the spread I had on the table for him and his cute nose wriggled in appreciation. "Wow, you have all my favorites!" He looked better to me than anything at the table when he rushed forward in his track pants with purple stripes and gave me a long kiss. When he broke the kiss, he stood back and patted his hand against my chest. "Thanks Max."

I didn't really know what to say. I was scared to really say what was on my mind because it seemed we had drifted apart. I came up with something on the fly. "I thought we could have a nice dinner, talk for a bit, and maybe watch some TV." I hesitated for a moment, I wasn't sure how he was going to react to my suggestion that we talk. I threw in the mention of TV at the last second, because there was now a big Samsung flat-screen in the great room.

Sam didn't reply to my suggestion, he took a seat and started carving up the turkey breast. I sat down beside him and he gave me three slices. As Sam piled up an alarming amount of the garlic mashed potatoes, he was beaming with happiness. "These potatoes are delicious, Max. Thanks!"

Since he helped me with the turkey, I poured him a glass of wine. Our dinner conversation was light, we mainly talked about our training. We talked about Morgan being alone. We were both worried about him and wanted him to be happy.

It was the perfect opportunity for me to bring up the state of our relationship. I tried for the most neutral segue I could think of to get him talking, I wanted to know what was on his mind because I wasn't happy with our situation. We learned during our officer training how to jump in and say what was on our mind. In a combat situation, it was imperative to get the facts and not be afraid to disagree if a plan was stupid. I hoped Sam wouldn't take offense. "Sam, you are a good person. I think it's awesome how much you care about my brother." I paused for a moment, feverishly trying to find a way to bring up what I wanted to talk about. "I was hoping that we could talk about you and me."

Sam's frown indicated he wasn't ready to talk about the two of us. "Max, I'm trying to work through it. I don't want to talk about it."

It wasn't what I wanted to hear, but I tried to be tactful. "Sam, I love you. We've been together since 1997. I'd like to have several more decades beyond that." I took a deep breath. "There isn't anyone else, I want you to know that."

His scowl indicated my comment was a bad one. "That's what all this is about isn't it?" He gestured at the table and the wine. "You think I'm being unfaithful?"

A tear leaked down my cheek. "I don't know what to think anymore."

That's where everything went to hell. Sam put his head in his hands like he had a bad headache. "Fuck!"

I sensed something wrong right away and knelt in front of him. "Sam, what's the matter?"

He shouted his reply, "My ears are ringing again. I can barely hear!" I could see he was in pain from his tears.

I felt bad for him, but I was still pissed. He assured me several times his ears weren't ringing anymore. I didn't know what to do. Fortunately, Jason appeared in his usual dramatic fashion and took matters in his own hands. He snapped his fingers and Sam was back in uniform. Jason turned to me, "You stay here. I'll take care of this."

Since I was brought up to take orders, I remained in my seat.

16

Jason was back in a flash and got to see me cry for the first time. He stood behind me and squeezed my shoulders as the sobs wracked my body. "Sam's okay, I took care of it. He's resting comfortably in the barracks since the training day is over."

"He told me he hasn't had any additional problems with his ears ringing."

Jason took my hand in his. "Sam is telling you the truth, Max. There's no need to worry, it's been taken care of."

"What do you mean by that?"

Jason shook his head. "I can't talk about it."

Sometimes Jason could infuriate me like no other. I stormed off to the great room. When that wasn't good enough, I went outside on the terrace. Jason was waiting for me. He was kicked back and comfortable in one of the loungers with a Coke on ice. There was a second glass waiting for me on the side table, in between two of the loungers, he looked over and grinned when I took a seat. "You know, all you have to do is say where you want to go. It's more efficient that way."

Our emissary from Upstairs was still on my nerves, but I took a seat and drank my Coke. "Something has changed between Sam and me and I don't know how to fix it."

"Max, the two of you have been together for about nine years. I know he loves you with all his heart. Sam is having a difficult time right now because he can't really tell anyone how much he loves you. Even though no one has asked, and the two of you certainly haven't told, many would say the two of you are breaking the law by even being in the military. That's something that Sam really struggles with and the fact the two of you can't have a relationship recognized by the government makes it worse. You have always been the strong one when it comes to that sort of thing, because of your family." Jason took a deep breath. "Sam compensates for those negatives by trying to be a bad-ass and keeping his feelings close to the vest. Even though I was gone for a few seconds, Sam and I had a long talk. He knows how much you love him."

I sensed a *but* coming somewhere, so I added it for him, "But…"

"Sam also knows you have feelings for Troy."

What the fuck? "Oh…" Since Jason seemed to know our secrets, I had to ask. "Doesn't he feel the same way about Dane?"

"Sam is attracted to him, but he knows your feelings for Troy are more substantial."

I was silent because I couldn't lie to Jason.

Jason squeezed my knee. "It's not your fault Max. You and Sam have done very well considering the obstacles that you have to deal with." He quirked a brow, "I'm pretty sure you and Troy realized you weren't just letting off some steam when it first happened."

I felt like such a shit. I felt horrible for being unfaithful to Sam and I felt even worse about the raging hard-on in my pants from remembering more than one excellent fucking that Troy had given me. One a scale of one-to-ten, they were about a thirty. I'd been telling myself it was an aberration since the first time. Sam clearly sensed it wasn't. I was at a loss with what to do about it. I turned in my chair and faced Jason. "I have no idea what I should do."

"The mansion and those who you love are inexorably linked. I think you should introduce Troy to its mysteries."

I was going to give Jason a piece of my mind, but I couldn't because the fucker promptly vanished. I looked up at the beautiful afternoon sky and voiced my frustration. "Morgan, I need you."

The Squirt appeared about three-seconds later, appropriately dressed in his swimming trunks. He was also carrying a fully loaded bong which he handed to me. "I think we need to get fucked up."

"Has Jason already given you the full briefing?"

Morgan smiled. "Jason has had a busy day, that's for sure. He told me everything." Then he gave me one hell of a scowl. "I don't understand why you have kept so much from me. You are my brother and I love you. Why wouldn't you mention your time with Troy to me? Why didn't you tell me that you and Sam had grown so far apart?"

I chose to stay away from discussing my sex life and brought up the reason I wanted him there instead. "Are you aware that Jason wants me to introduce the house to Troy?"

Morgan nodded. "Seems fair to me, Max."

I shook my head. "Morgan, I love Sam. We've hit a rough patch. I don't want to bring Troy in the middle of this any more than he is already. If I bring him to the mansion, that would be like casting Sam aside. I can't do that to him."

Morgan sat the pipe down after we each had a hit, because Jason tended to go for the strong stuff. We needed to focus more on the discussion at hand instead of getting any higher. He reached out and squeezed my shoulder. "Max, you have got to quit tearing yourself up over having sex with Troy. You were both in Afghanistan. You just came back from battling insurgents and needed each other. Sam wasn't spending much time with you. I think you can still love Sam even though Troy fucked you like a boss."

I felt guilty as hell for what I had done with Troy, but I couldn't suppress my giggle for my brother's word choice.

Morgan smiled for a moment and then became deadly serious. "Max, Sam is pulling away from you because he's in pain. The ringing in his ears is classic PTSD." He shook his head sadly. "It's no wonder, he's been through some serious shit. He has a scar on his cheek to prove it." Morgan shifted in his seat so that he was facing me, he put his hands on my knees when I turned to face him. "If you want to save your relationship with Sam, both of you need to get out of the Army and try to have a normal life. I only hope it isn't already too late."

"Morgan, we are almost finished with our training, the Army is going to require us to serve at least six more years because of the time and money they have spent on us."

My brother was more serious than I have ever seen him. "They will be more than happy to show you the door if you and Sam acknowledge your relationship."

It was hard for me to counter that, so I only had one weak argument. "Do you know what that would do to Dad?"

Morgan's expression was stern. "He will be disappointed with Uncle Sam, not you."

"I don't think I could get Sam to agree. If I outed both of us without his permission, he would probably never talk to me again."

Morgan stood and started to pace. I had the feeling he was going to say something pretty heavy, so I stayed quiet. My brother had always been one of the most important people in my life and I would listen to everything he had to say. After a few moments, he spoke. "Max, would you rather have him pissed at you or dead? He shouldn't go back into combat in his condition. He needs to come back here and have a normal life. He's pulling away from you because he's afraid something is going to happen to him, or to you. Stop being so ridiculous and come back here so we can enjoy our lives together."

"Morgan, I promise I will really think about it. I need to talk to Sam and see what he has to say."

Morgan gave me a hug that almost squeezed the life out of me. "Go back and talk to him."

When I jumped back to the barracks, I was back in uniform and came out of the latrine like I had just taken a piss. Sam was in his bunk next to mine cleaning his rifle. He looked up and smiled when I sat down beside him. I smiled back at him. "How are you feeling?"

"Pretty good actually. Jason made the ringing go away instantly." Sam reached out and discreetly squeezed my arm. "How's the Squirt?"

"Feisty as ever."

Sam laughed and then he looked at me in a way that he hadn't for months. "Let's go back to the mansion."

I was instantly hard as a rock. "Okay…"

When we got to the mansion, we were in our usual room.

Sam came up to me and promptly kissed me breathless. "Max, I love you. I'm sorry that things have been so tough between us." He took off his shirt. "Baby, I need you."

I'm sure my eyes were wide as saucers. "Okay, sounds like a plan." I took my shirt off too.

We were both completely naked in record time. I gaped at him for a moment because he looked good enough to eat. I reached out and played with his dick, which was already at attention, like a good soldier. I smiled. "God you are so hot."

Sam grinned at me. "Are you stoned?"

"Yeah, I guess I am. I smoked a bowl with Morgan when we were here, I guess the effects are back since I haven't been gone that long."

Sam stepped forward on top of my feet and smiled. "Look at that, now I'm two inches taller."

He hadn't done that in years. It took my breath away because it reminded me of the dreams I had a long time ago. I still couldn't believe we'd been together for so long.

Sam snapped his fingers and the pipe and a lighter appeared in his hand. He gave me a grin for the first time in ages. "I'm gonna catch up."

I arched a brow, smiled, and stroked his dick some more. "Okay, go ahead. I've got something here to keep me busy." Sam took a hit and reached out and played with my dick too. I wiggled my toes under his feet because he was still standing on mine, we both laughed.

Sam took another hit off the pipe and kissed me. He shotgunned his hit into my mouth, we hadn't ever done before. I could tell our time together was going to be intense. Sam dropped to his knees. Before he took me into his mouth, he looked up and smiled. "I'm gonna suck your brains out."

I tousled his hair. "Go ahead, I'm not sure I have any brain cells left."

After a few minutes of some of the most decadent slurping and popping I'd ever heard, I pushed him off of me. "Stop, I'm gonna die if I don't get to suck you right now."

Sam stood and took me by the hand and led me towards the bed. "That's why they invented the sixty-nine."

I had a better idea. I hadn't manhandled him in a long time. I reached out, picked him up, and turned him upside down. I took his cock in my mouth.

Sam laughed out loud. "Oh my God, that is hot." Then he went back down on me. I always got such a charge out of carrying him around. I couldn't believe I hadn't done that maneuver sooner.

Sam was smaller than me, but he was still heavy after a few minutes. He'd bulked up substantially over the years. I managed to carry him over to the bed where we fell into it without breaking contact. I wrapped my arms around his mid-section and continued sucking like I hadn't tasted him in years. It was perfect; his taste, his smell, and his enthusiasm were almost more than I could take. I started to wonder if Jason had blasted him with some kind of horny-ray or something. It was almost like the years were erased and we were sophomores in college again.

I spread his legs and went for his balls. They were drawn up nice and tight. I laved them with my tongue and easily fit both into my mouth.

I knew Sam liked it when my finger eased into his opening. I've always liked that and intended to give him what he wanted, but I had another idea forming in my head. I pulled his legs back, exposing his hole and leaned in for a good lick.

"Unghh…"

I smiled while I licked. "You like that, huh?"

"Un-huh."

Poor guy, couldn't do much talking when my dick was still in his mouth.

I was ready for something different, for the first time in a long time, I wanted his ass. I moved him into position and looked at him for a moment.

Sam had a mischievous grin, "This is a treat, I love it when you fuck me."

I reached for the lube and coated a finger. When I eased my finger in his tight ass, I smiled. "I think this might be kind of fun."

Sam was impossibly tight, very enthusiastic with the preparations, and shockingly loud when I curled my finger just right and pushed his magic button over and over. There was no way I could suppress my giggle. He scrunched up his face. "Damn, that's awesome! Give me another finger, babe."

It would have been impossible for me not to do what he wanted. I wanted to make sure he was good and ready, so I kept up the pressure with my two fingers and gave him another blowjob to keep him happy. After a couple of minutes of that, I leaned over and gave him a nice hickey on his hip bone and left teeth marks on the inside of his thigh. He always was a tasty guy. By the time I was done, he was panting and begging for me to fuck him.

I got more lube and got myself good and slick. "So how do you want to do this?"

"I want to ride you."

I smiled. Our Army training did such a nice job of making our communication simple and direct. I sat down on the bed and patted my lap, "Here you go."

I preferred it when he faced me when we were doing that sort of thing, but the mechanics were always better when his back was to me, or more often, with my back to him. It was a nice change though. I sucked in a breath at the initial breach. It felt so good, I buried my head in his shoulder and bit him. I wrapped my arms around him tightly and peppered the back of his neck and shoulders with light kisses. After a few minutes, I got flat on my back and pulled him down against me. It was time for me to do some of the work. I flexed my hips and gave him a thorough pounding. Since my right hand was still fairly slick, I stroked his hard dick. It was much better that way. I loved having all his weight on me.

Sam was close. I could feel his channel start to tighten. I jacked him harder and nibbled on his ear. Sam let out a roar and shot an amazing load on his chest. Some of it splattered on his shoulder and I helpfully licked it off before my dick erupted in his ass. I pumped into him through the duration of our shockwave and we collapsed into a pile of tangled limbs.

We barely managed a quick clean up before we dozed off. We shared a kiss and a quick, "I love you," before we were fast asleep.

I was so happy. Everything seemed normal again.

17

October 11, 2006

Our training group was extra motivated; we had one final task before we officially graduated as leaders of a Special Forces detachment in four days. It wasn't horribly complicated, we had to run through a simulated mission where we would ride in on helicopters, fast-rope to the ground, and storm a remote, heavily-defended camp in the woods.

I was nervous as we made our preparations and the helicopters landed. When Sam and I woke up from our time together at the mansion, he seemed so happy and relaxed, I decided not to bring up the discussion Morgan and I had earlier. I felt we gained some new ground, and even though we would probably be in separate countries, I was relaxed in the knowledge we still had the mansion and could jump there anytime we wanted. I could tell things were better between us, so I decided to tuck my misgivings neatly away and not worry. I needed to get my head in the game because training missions in the Special Forces could quickly become dangerous if you weren't paying attention.

Dane's squad took off in the first helicopter. Moments later, Sam took off with his squad in the second. Troy and I were hunched down towards the ground to avoid the rotor blast. When Sam's squad reached altitude, mine was the next on the list.

It was an excellent day for our training mission. It was a little cloudy with a slight breeze, but well within operational parameters.

As Sam's helicopter was lifting into the air, there was a sudden, strong gust of wind. Since I lived in Colorado, near the mountains, I was used to an occasional strong gust here and there. It was definitely some sort of wind shear. I was nervous, but Special Forces pilots were the best in the business.

I looked up at the helicopter and my nervousness turned into sheer terror when I saw it tilt to the side. Everything beyond that point was a bit of a blur. It was nothing like the movies. It was very quick. The helicopter canted over further and dropped like a stone.

Troy saw everything unfold right beside me. He wasn't rooted in place with shock like me. He grabbed my arm and shouted, "Run!"

We weren't fast enough.

A tremendous explosion sent Troy and me face-first into the ground. The rain of debris and shrapnel was murderous. I felt a stab of pain along the back of my leg and I heard, and felt, the bone in my arm snap when it smashed into a large rock on the ground.

Everything went white…

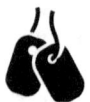

When I came to, I was sitting in a huge ornate room. I wasn't in the mansion, but I knew I was somewhere Upstairs. I was seated at the table with Jason by my side.

Jason looked at me sadly as he snapped his fingers for the Cokes and glasses of ice. He poured the first glass and handed it to me. "Have a drink, Max. I'm sure you know why you are here."

"Am I dead?"

Jason shook his head. "No."

I swallowed around the lump in my throat, I knew how bad the explosion was. I decided to prolong the inevitable and glared at Jason. "I thought you said they don't have Coke up here."

"I raised a big stink about it and now we do."

I started crying. "Sam's dead isn't he?"

Jason nodded slowly. "Maxwell, I'm so sorry, Sam perished in the crash."

Cold, deep fury settled in the pit of my stomach. I was so mad at myself for not having the conversation with Sam that I should have after we made love. Jason was the next best target for my anger, I jumped out of my chair and pointed at him. "You fucker! You are the one that killed him!" I stalked off to the other side of the room, crying the entire way.

Jason pulled me into an embrace. "Maxwell, I'm so sorry. I stopped the ringing in his ears, but there was nothing else I could do." He hugged me even tighter. "I know this will be difficult for you to hear, but I hope you can find some comfort in the knowledge there is an afterlife and that Sam is happy, safe, and in a good place."

I wasn't quite ready to give in yet. "You shouldn't have interfered, if you would have let the ringing go on, Sam would have been discharged for PTSD and he would still be alive."

Jason stepped back. "You know it doesn't work that way. When it's someone's time, that's it." He held up his hand to stop my inevitable question. "At my level, I have no idea when that time is. I'm as shocked as you are."

I started crying again. "What the hell do I do now? Everything was getting better and now he's gone!" I glared at Jason again. "Wait, did you have something to do with our last time? Was that why it was so good?"

Jason pulled me close and hugged me again. "No, that was all you and him." He patted me on the back, "I can do a lot of things, but I can't make people horny."

I suddenly remembered Sam wasn't the only one involved. "Oh my God, what about Troy? Where's Dane? Are they all right?"

"The three of you are going to be okay." Jason cleared his throat, "Max, you know how things work up here, I can't keep you long."

Typical. My nose flared like it always did when Jason didn't want to give me any answers.

Jason took a seat in one of the chairs and pointed at one of the others. "Sit, I still have a minute or two and there are important details I need to share. You already know the afterlife exists, so that will help you more than you know. The three of you have a long road ahead. When you recover, you need to remember that your mission at the house isn't complete." He stood and his expression was more like my dad and less like his usual playful self. "Do I have your word that you won't let me down?"

"Can I see Sam one more time?"

Jason pursed his lips. "You know stuff like that isn't allowed."

I sighed. "Jason, I'm so tired of it all. I'm not sure if I ever want to go to that house again. I want a normal life."

Jason's expression softened. "Maxwell, you won't be alone. You have Morgan, Troy, and Dane to help you get through it. We'll speak again soon. I'm confident we can come up with a plan that will work for everyone."

"Okay…"

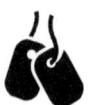

My brother was sitting in a chair beside my bed when I came to. I knew it was him before I even woke up because he had hold of my hand. His touch is what brought me back to consciousness and my squeeze is what let him know I was coming around.

He stood up and kissed me on the forehead. "Welcome back, Max."

"Hey." I cleared my throat. "I need something to drink."

"I'll call the nurse."

I wasn't sure where the hell I was, but I was able to confirm I was in a military hospital when the nurse came in, she was a captain like me. She handed me a Styrofoam cup that was way too small for my level of thirst. "Welcome back, Captain. Start off with small sips and we'll get you a larger drink if your stomach tolerates it. It's a standard precaution, you had a concussion."

I looked at the cast on my arm. It was my left. Since I was right-handed, I'd still be able to write—among other things.

Morgan looked at me sadly and put down his magazine. "Max, I'm so sorry. Jason sent me here, he told me everything." He wiped his eyes against his shoulder.

"Have you talked to Mom and Dad?"

Morgan checked his watch. "They should be here in another hour or so." He grinned, "Dad ordered me to stay put, they are taking a cab from the airport."

"Where are we?"

"We're in the hospital, dumb ass."

I chuckled. It was nice to see my brother had his sense of humor. "I was asking you if we are still on Fort Bragg, numb nuts."

Morgan's eyes twinkled. "Yes"

I needed to know about the others. "Do you know how Troy is doing? Have you seen Dane? He was already in the air…"

"I have no idea. Nobody will tell me anything." Morgan brightened slightly, "Maybe Mom and Dad will get some answers. They intimidate the hell out of everyone."

I appreciated his attempts to be funny, but I needed to ask him something important. "Do you know where Sam's body is?"

Morgan had done a good job so far, but he lost it when I mentioned Sam. I squeezed his hand as his body heaved with sobs. "They took him to Dover." Morgan's sobs continued, I wasn't looking forward to hearing what was next, but on an intellectual level, I knew. The explosion had been a bad one. "Max, his parents have been notified." He choked up some more. "They are having him cremated."

I quickly drained the rest of my water. I couldn't think of anything else to say after hearing information like that. All I could do was stare off in space. I was glad I had Morgan with me or I would have truly fallen apart.

18

I managed to sleep through the night. When I woke the next morning, Mom and Dad were in the room with me. We exchanged hugs and bawled our eyes out until we were gasping for breath. I looked around the room, "Where's Squirt?"

Dad smiled, he always got such a charge out of Morgan's nickname. "He's back at the hotel getting some rest."

Mom gave me a thorough briefing about my injuries. My left arm was fractured and already in a cast. My left leg had 126 stitches on the back side from shrapnel wounds. I also had a deep laceration on my neck that came frighteningly close to my jugular.

Mom reached out and took my hand. "You are going to be here for a few days before they let you out. Your father and I will stay here with you as long as you need."

"You don't have to do that."

Dad sat forward in his chair. "We've done plenty of traveling. You are our priority."

"When does Morgan have to go back?"

Mom smiled, "I have no idea; sometimes it's impossible to get an answer out of him. He'll probably stay here until you are discharged from the hospital."

I looked up and winked at my mom. "If you go for both armpits at the same time, he'll tell you anything you want to know."

Mom laughed. "Thanks, I'll keep that in mind."

"Mom, how are Troy and Dane?"

"They are going to be okay," Mom said. "Troy came very close to losing his left kidney from being impaled by debris. They had him in surgery for seven hours. He's going to be here for a few days himself."

"And Dane?"

Dad answered for her. "Dane wasn't injured, he's with the rest of the training class. They are confined to barracks and being monitored for PTSD."

I remembered Jason's promise. He told me I would have my family, along with Troy and Dane, at my side so we could fulfill our destiny with the house. There was one problem, none of us had injuries that would end our careers. I'm pretty sure that was the precise moment when I decided we had been through enough. Maybe Morgan was right, if I told them I was gay, they would send me home. That still didn't take care of Troy and Dane.

I had a lot to think about.

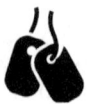

Four days later, I had a visit from a serious-looking major. Mom and Dad were at the hotel getting some rest. Morgan was in the cafeteria getting something to eat.

The major was from the Adjutant General's office. I could tell by the insignia on his uniform. He had a huge stack of paperwork with him. He got down to business right away, "Captain Maxwell Carter?"

"Yes Sir, I'm Captain Carter."

The Major let out an audible sigh. "There's no pleasant way to start this discussion, so I'll just get on with it." He cleared his throat, "In accordance with DOD Directive 1304.26, your commission has been rescinded, effective on your date of discharge from this hospital."

My blood turned cold, I knew the directive had to do with the Army's *Don't Ask, Don't Tell* policy. I was very surprised because there was no way anyone could have any evidence linking Sam and me. I got a little mouthy with the major, since I was being showed the door—after being injured in the line of duty. "Do what you have to do, but leave my boyfriend's name out of this. He's dead, he doesn't deserve to have his name drug through the mud."

The Major looked puzzled. "Captain Atherton is alive and well, down the hall. He is receiving a similar notification this very moment." The way he shook his head was a sure sign of his disagreement with Army policy. "The AG is having a busy day." He looked at me sort of strangely, "You seem to have had an inordinate number of gay men in your training class, Captain. We're processing three different officers out today."

I barely repressed my smile, it appeared Jason had been busy taking care of things for me. For the first time I felt relaxed. I was so relieved I didn't have to take steps to force Troy and Dane back to Colorado with me. I had been worrying about it for hours. Since I wasn't a captain in the Army anymore, I decided to give the major a hard time. I gave him a Boy Scout salute. "Thanks, you are dismissed."

The Major looked like he was going to chew a piece of my ass. At the last moment, his expression softened. "Captain, between you and me, I think this decision is complete bullshit." He reached out and shook my hand. "From one officer to another, I appreciate your service. Your record is outstanding and you should be proud of your accomplishments. There aren't many who are able to get into Special Forces." He handed me his card. "If you have any questions, please don't hesitate to call me."

Morgan came back to the room about fifteen minutes later. He noticed my expression, somewhere in-between pissed and relieved. "What happened?"

"Looks like I'm coming home, Squirt."

He didn't jump for joy like I thought he would, in fact his voice was completely neutral. "Are you being kicked out?"

I nodded. "Because of my homosexual relationship with Troy Atherton, can you believe that?"

Morgan was way too quiet as he shuffled his feet. Oh yes, he was guilty as hell. I narrowed my gaze. "Why do you look like the cat that ate the canary?"

"Well…"

"Morgan…" I practically growled.

Morgan fidgeted in place for a moment. Then he took a deep breath and let it out. "Look Max, I was operating on strict orders from Jason."

"Just tell me what you did."

The answer left his mouth, almost in a whisper. "I told them about you, Troy, and Dane."

More than anything, I was relieved. I reached for his hand and he bent down and hugged me. I still reminded him who was boss though. "I won't kick your ass this time."

The nurse came in the room. It was time for me to get out of bed and walk around. I turned to my brother. "If you don't mind, I'm going to check in on Troy."

Troy was two rooms over from mine. He was lying on his stomach. He smiled when I entered the room, which was a good sign. Maybe he wasn't too pissed about being kicked out after all. "Look at you, up and moving around."

"How much longer are you going to be in here?"

Troy grimaced, "At least a few more days. You know how Uncle Sam is, he doesn't give any details until he's damn good and ready."

"I need to talk to you about my visit from the AG."

Troy nodded and smiled. "Yeah, they came and talked to me too."

"You don't seem that upset."

Troy took a deep breath. "Well...It's kind of hard to explain."

The situation definitely had Jason Buchanan written all over it. Since he already had Morgan take care of his dirty work, it wasn't much of a stretch for him to have eased the way with Troy. A dream perhaps? That was first thought to rush into my head. A typical Jason Buchanan maneuver. "Go ahead and tell me. You're about to discover all is not what it seems."

Troy looked at me like I might be weird for a moment.

I decided to help him along. "Did you have a dream?"

Troy worried his lip for a moment before answering. "How did you know?"

I grinned as I reached out and took his hand. "I want to show you something." I mouthed the magic word. I wasn't entirely sure if we could jump while injured. It seemed reasonable to me if we could smoke pot at the mansion and not be stoned when we jumped back to the real world, then it should work the other way—with wounds instead of marijuana.

Troy and I ended up on the terrace, it was a beautiful sunny day.

Troy's eyes were huge as he took in our surroundings. "Holy shit! What the fuck is this? We're not injured!"

We were conveniently in our swimming suits. I had my orange board shorts and Troy was wearing a green pair. I steered him over to one of the lounge chairs. "Would you like something to drink?"

"Do you have any beer?"

I nodded. "Anything in particular?"

"I don't care, whatever you have will be great." He looked sort of shell-shocked.

I snapped my fingers and the bottle appeared in my hands. I got myself my usual Coke.

I let Troy soak it all in for a few minutes before I said anything. I forced myself not to pay too much attention to his body, since so much was on display. It was neither the time nor place for that sort of thing. Truthfully, I wasn't sure I would ever be interested in another guy again. It didn't seem right.

I must have gotten wrapped up in my thoughts, because Troy had to squeeze my leg. "Do you want to hear what he told me?"

"I hope Jason was polite and introduced himself."

Troy grinned, "He told me to come to Boulder when I got out of the hospital. He said we would all be together, and we would be able to provide a place for veterans to learn a new skill and be around supportive people who could help them adjust to civilian life."

I looked at Troy in amazement and gave some added snark for Jason's benefit. "Really? It was nice of him to tell someone about his plans." It was certainly news to me.

We both flinched when Jason suddenly appeared at the end of my lounger in his swimming suit. He looked at me and winked, "Thanks Sport, I can take it from here."

He took a dive in the pool before I could hurl a few choice words his way. I looked at Troy, "Be prepared, Jason could try the patience of a saint." I grinned as I imagined he probably had.

Troy looked a little dazed, but he gave me a weak smile and took a healthy sip of his beer.

Jason came out of the pool a few minutes later. His grin was broad, "Sorry guys, I miss the pool."

I looked him over critically. He was wearing a sixties-era swim suit. It was thoughtful of him to give me such handy ammunition, "That has to be the ugliest swim suit I have ever seen." It would have been much better if he had on a loose pair like Troy and me. I could see his entire dick because suits from that era were tight.

Jason snapped his fingers and he was completely naked. "Is this better?"

Troy laughed when Jason turned around so we could see him from all sides.

I put my hand over my eyes. "Dude, put something on."

Jason snapped his fingers again and he was suddenly wearing a red pair of shorts like ours. He sat on the end of my lounger again. "Is this better for your delicate sensibilities?"

I had a valid reason. "Jason, Troy and I are twenty-nine years old. You are still in your seventeen-year-old body. Think about it for a minute."

Jason squeezed my knee. "Sorry, I forgot you are such a Puritan." Then he grinned, "Technically I'm your mother's age."

I shook my head. "Yeah, you're definitely not helping with the *ick* factor."

Troy sat sideways on his lounger and joined us in our little huddle. He looked Jason over in amazement. "I can't believe you are real."

Jason patted him on the knee. "I'm going to give you the briefing now." He looked over to me before he continued, I guess he was waiting for me to nod my approval, so I did.

Like it mattered…

Troy's briefing was much longer and more comprehensive than any of mine had been. It lasted for almost two hours. Troy took in every word without comment, only stopping Jason twice because he needed another beer. Jason finally showed him how to snap his fingers and get his own. It was cute to see him flustered from the interruptions.

Jason went over absolutely everything—the history of the house, what happened to him, how Morgan and I discovered the place and how Sam and I managed to be together for so long without ever living together.

Jason took us into the kitchen at one point and made us sandwiches, explaining he wanted to do it the real way to keep busy.

After Troy finished his excellent turkey and bacon sandwich, Jason asked, "Do you have any questions with what I've told you so far?"

Troy shook his head. It was amazing he was taking it all in so well. Sort of like it was part of his destiny. That wouldn't be strange at all.

Jason wasn't finished with the questioning. "Troy, will you be able to help us accomplish our mission?"

"I can teach veterans auto repair and anything to do with growing plants and landscaping." He looked over at me, "I could probably help with the woodworking too. You guys taught me a lot when I was here before."

Jason seemed satisfied. "Excellent. Dane has a gift when it comes to animals and he's good at sanding too." Jason smiled at me and winked. "I think everything is starting to come together."

I had one teensy little question. "Um, the woodworking isn't going to be that big of a problem, we have the equipment for that." I shook my head. "How are we going to do the rest? It's going to cost a lot of money for landscaping equipment, not to mention auto shop tools."

Jason gave me one of his typical looks like I didn't have a single functioning brain cell in my head. "You have to know by now that we've thought of that." He started to pace, "We've had people working on this for a long time." He clapped his hands together, "This has been a very productive session. The two of you need to concentrate on healing and I will take care of everything else."

He vanished before I could say a word.

I smiled at Troy. "Welcome to the show…"

19

October 2006

Troy and I were discharged from the hospital nine days after the accident. Mom and Dad rented a minivan; the captain's chairs in the rear made it the most comfortable way to accommodate all of us. Troy made it clear he was coming with me because his parents didn't even know he was injured. I only knew a few basics about his family because Troy never liked to talk about it. All I knew was they had a huge blowout about his being gay after he graduated college. Mom and Dad were delighted to have someone else to take under their wing and be supportive of.

Mom, Dad, and Morgan decided to take turns, which really meant Dad let them drive for precisely one hour each. Morgan hung out in the back with Troy and me. I stayed pretty quiet for the first leg of our journey. Dad took I-40 out of North Carolina. We were going to try to make it to Nashville the first day—as long as the ibuprofen held out, Troy and I were still pretty uncomfortable from our injuries.

My grief over Sam was almost like a freight train, it came barreling through on a regular schedule. Sometimes it was a few tears as I looked at the scenery, thinking how Sam would have liked it.

Other times, it was much worse. Morgan was awesome, he held my hand or hugged me whenever I lost it. Troy was great too, he probably held my hand for at least two hundred miles; or had his hand on my shoulder or my knee.

Since we were traveling with old people, we stopped at full service sit-down restaurants when it was time to eat. Mom and Morgan ate like civilians—at a normal pace. Dad and I ate fast because Uncle Sam taught us to. Troy didn't have much of an appetite at all.

Since Dad and I finished up at the same time, he looked over at me and smiled. "Do you want to go outside and get some fresh air?"

I nodded. I had a feeling he was in the mood for a private discussion. More than likely it would be related somehow to you-know-who.

My suspicions were confirmed once we were outside. "Max, I'd like to talk to you about something." He paused a moment and shook his head, "I'm not sure how to start, because you are going to think I'm crazy."

I'd never felt so relieved in my entire life. "Trust me, there isn't anything you could say that would make me think you're crazy."

Dad fidgeted and eventually waded into it. "Have you and your brother ever heard of someone named Jason Buchanan?"

I played it cool. "Morgan mentioned his name once. He was that kid who was killed back in the sixties. I've heard the house where they lived is haunted."

Dad grew more stern. "Have you or your brother even been to that house?"

There was no point in lying, the plausibility of being grounded seemed comfortably remote, so I told the truth with a quick nod.

Dad was now in full drill-sergeant mode. "Even though I specifically instructed you and your brother never to step one single foot in that house?"

I shrugged. "Dad, that was like an engraved invitation. What did you expect?"

"I expected my orders to be followed to the letter, that's what I expected!"

There was obviously more to the story, or my dad wouldn't have brought up Jason's name. "Dad, what's this about?"

The words came out of my dad's mouth in a rush. "I saw Jason Buchanan walking along Pearl Street the day before he died."

I couldn't resist, "How old were you at the time?" I already had a pretty good idea because I wasn't that horrible at math.

"I was nine."

My expression was one of triumph. "Ha! You mean to tell me your parents let you *wander* around Pearl Street *aimlessly* when you were so young?" Aimless wandering was one of Dad's favorite expressions when Morgan and I were growing up. It was why we were never allowed to go anywhere unsupervised until we were well into high school.

Dad glared at me for a moment. "Maxwell..."

It was time to get to the meat of the discussion. "Did you know Jason?"

Dad nodded. "Yes, his family always threw a big party every summer for kids in the area." Dad smiled at a happy memory, "They were always a load of fun. We got to go horseback riding and swimming in their pool."

"Did you and Jason talk often?"

Dad nodded. "For some reason, he always seemed to take a special interest in me. He always went out of his way to ask me how I was doing." Dad was smiling again. "Believe me, it was a big deal because Jason was eight years older than me."

I was getting antsy. "Dad, did Jason say something to you the last time you saw him?"

"He told me I would have two sons someday and I should love them no matter what."

I was shocked into silence. How long had Jason been involved with my family? Suddenly, I had another more urgent question. "Has Jason spoken to you recently?"

Dad didn't bat an eye at my question. "I dreamt about him the night before your accident."

I sighed. Why was it so difficult to get answers from people? "And what did he say?"

Dad looked at me with the kindest expression imaginable. "Son, he told me everything."

"Everything?"

Dad nodded. "It explained a lot. Your mom and I have been really worried about you." He appeared to be searching for the best way to put what he had to say in actual words. "I had no idea you and Sam were able to be together so much while you were in the Army." He placed his hand on my shoulder. "I understand how upset you have been." He shook his head in disbelief, "And here, I was convinced you two weren't even together anymore."

"What about Mom?"

Dad looked worried. "She has been strangely quiet about it."

"I find it hard to believe you haven't talked to her." It didn't seem like a good time to parrot one of his frequent lectures about the value of good communication.

"I don't need my wife thinking I'm crazy." He looked at me cross-eyed. "She's a psychiatrist…"

Dad's humor was a relief, so I tried to allay his concern. "What if Jason talked to her and she's worried you might think she's nuts?"

Dad nodded. "You're probably right."

"Dad, I appreciate you telling me. I know what to do."

Morgan, Troy, and I had a quick chat before we got back in the van.

Once we were all seated, Morgan and I mouthed the magic word. We didn't know if Mom and Dad would be able to come along or not. We took a leap of faith, because what else could we do?

I was fairly certain there hadn't been so many people in the mansion for decades. Since the jumping process usually had a mind of its own, we ended up in the conservatory. Troy was in heaven and immediately started fussing over the plants.

Mom let out a gasp. "Oh my God, it was real!"

I went to her and hugged her. "You aren't crazy Mom. Jason talked to you in your dreams, that's why he allowed you to be here."

Mom looked around and noticed my arm, "Your arm is healed!" She looked over to Troy, who was obviously feeling better than he had in days. She shook her head in amazement.

Morgan took her by the hand. "Come on, let's go to the great room. You should probably sit down for this."

I decided to show Mom some of the powers of the house. "Would you like something to drink?"

She nodded slowly. "I'd give anything for a lot of bourbon right now."

I snapped my fingers, the full tumbler appeared in my hand and I gave it to her. She downed every drop and handed it back to me. "Hit me again."

Dad and the others had beer. I had a margarita on the rocks because I was in the mood for something different. The others gazed longingly at my drink, so I had to get more for them too.

Mom seemed to be taking it very well. "Are we in Heaven?"

"We like to refer to it as Upstairs."

Leave it to Jason to appear at the most dramatic moment. He snapped his fingers and had a margarita of his own. Jason looked up at the ceiling. It looked like he was receiving a message from his superiors. He nodded and said, "As you wish." He winked at me and snapped his fingers again.

It took a moment to catalogue all the differences. We were still in the mansion, but it was noticeably different. For one thing, it didn't seem nearly as large. The furnishings were more modern, and the interior wasn't as snazzy as the version upstairs—more Ethan Allen, less Versailles.

Troy smiled when he looked towards the conservatory, it was still there, but completely empty. It was like a blank canvas waiting for his artistic talents. It took my breath away when I saw how happy it made him.

"We are back in real time," Jason explained.

Mom the realist, interjected. "We can't leave the van sitting in Tennessee, the rental company will charge us a fortune."

Jason smiled at her. "Don't worry, it's already taken care of. Your luggage is in the foyer." Jason turned to my dad. "John, I'm so glad to see you again." He gestured at me and Morgan. "You should be very proud how your two boys have turned out."

Dad went to Jason and gave him a hug. It was a touching moment.

Jason took a seat on the edge of the coffee table and the rest of us sat on the couches that flanked it. He snapped his fingers and a mammoth pile of paperwork suddenly appeared. Jason smiled at me and the guys. "Are you guys ready?"

"Ready for what?" Troy asked.

"To fulfill your promises," Jason reminded gently.

I looked at him when I had an important thought. "What about Dane? Shouldn't he be here too?"

Jason shook his head. "Well damn…" He disappeared in a flash and returned just as quickly with Dane. It didn't take too long to explain things to him. Jason had obviously been at work, behind the scenes, with him as well. After Dane got a beer and had some idea of what was going on, we were ready to proceed.

Jason turned to my mother. "Karen, we're going to need your help too."

"What kind of help?" She asked.

Jason grinned at her. "Are you still a psychiatrist like I asked?"

Mom nodded.

The rest of us were stunned. I spoke first, "How long have you two been talking?"

Mom squeezed my knee. "Since I was a little girl. I never said anything because I didn't want you to think I was crazy."

Dad huffed a breath. "Holy shit."

Mom laughed out loud. "Jason and I were the same age." She smiled at him. "We were both nine-years-old at the time. When a little boy tells you matter-of-factly you are going to be a doctor when you grow up, you pay attention." She patted Jason on the knee. "And you did a very nice job of reinforcing it through the years." Mom's gaze swiveled back to me. "I had a feeling something was up with you kids." She alternated back-and-forth between me and my brother, "Your grades went up dramatically after starting college, when most students get worse." She narrowed her gaze at Jason like I would've done. I was so proud of her. "You've obviously been involved with them for a long time."

It was such a relief. It took over an hour to go through everything with her. We hugged and cried several times throughout the story. She completely understood how close Sam and I really were.

Jason looked on happily and began to lay out his vision. He wanted us to work with gay soldiers in order to permanently remove the stain from the property as quickly as possible. My name, in addition to Morgan's, Troy's, and Dane's, would all be on the deed. He gave Morgan a checkbook and told him the account would have money in it for what we needed, until we didn't need it anymore.

Mom would help with counseling and act as a medical director, so we would get certified and be able to accept insurance and work with the VA. Dad would set up a workshop and help out where needed. Drill Sergeants were especially well-suited when it came to counseling and Jason expected Dad to help Mom.

I would need to do some traveling from time to time because it would be my job to go to those in need, interview them, and bring them back to Boulder. Morgan would act as a backup and work with those who were interested in a career in programming.

Dad practically sobbed with joy when Jason led us into the wood shop. It would be big enough to handle the most ambitious of projects. It wasn't full of equipment yet, because Jason knew we already had most of what was needed. Dad always wanted to get into making solid-wood entry doors and garage doors. Now he could because we had the money, and the room, to do it.

One-third of the building was empty and closed off from the workshop. Jason explained the area could be used as expansion for the shop or as an area for Troy to work on auto repairs.

The outside of the house was fully restored, it was simpler than the exterior I was used to, but still impressive. There was still a lot to do with the landscaping, but none of us were afraid of hard work.

I was concerned. "I hope you didn't snap your fingers and get all this done overnight. People would notice something like that."

Jason put his arm around my waist. "The renovations took eight months and all of you were gone the entire time. We used local contractors for everything." His hand landed on my ass. "You realize I'm not some dumb kid, don't you?"

I took his hand and placed it in a more appropriate spot. "Thanks, Jason."

Jason ushered all of us back inside. We ended up in the kitchen because we were all hungry. Mom, Dad, and Jason busied themselves putting dinner together. They ordered the rest of us out of the room, so we decided to go out on the terrace and get stoned. We were adults, it wasn't like we were going to get in trouble with Mom and Dad.

When dinner was over, we cleared the table. Jason left the room and came back carrying a contract that was ridiculously thick—at least four inches. His expression turned serious. "I need all of you to sign this. Once your signatures are on this document, this property will be yours and you can start helping those in need with a little help from me now and then. I will still check in with you occasionally if I'm needed."

I thought about giving him some grief about the thickness of the contract, but I knew it wouldn't do any good. I didn't think twice about it. I was actually happy because it guaranteed future snark with Jason. I knew he would probably come down at some point, say something ridiculous and assure me it was covered in section 4,280, paragraph eight, sub-section Q.

After we all signed, Jason pulled out an impressive gold stamp from his pocket and notarized it. Then, as usual, he promptly vanished. Dane was gone too. Jason abducted him from Oregon and he needed to spend some time with his family.

I sure was happy I had mine.

20

Late 2006

It took some time for me to get with the program. I didn't do a whole lot for the first couple of weeks after we were back in Colorado. I needed time to heal. Troy and I didn't hop right into bed either. Both of us needed time to process everything that had happened.

Dane arrived about two weeks after we got to Colorado. The Army flew him home to Oregon and he needed to spend some time with his family. When he arrived in Boulder, he seemed refreshed and ready to talk about the future.

Since my Mom was one hell of a psychiatrist, I spent a lot of time on her couch. Sometimes we would talk for three or four hours at a time. Sometimes, for a change of scenery, she had me get in the car with her so we could go for a ride in the mountains or go down into Denver to her favorite mall. A little bit of retail therapy can do wonders for a damaged soul.

I spent a lot of time with Dad out in the shop. He was up to his eyeballs in orders, so I was more than happy to get my mind off of the emptiness in my heart and get to work. Troy was at my side for all of it, not only was he a great friend, he was one hell of a worker. His shoulder was at the perfect height to cry on, too. I did a lot of it those first few weeks.

I bawled my eyes out one day when Troy asked if I would like to go to Burger King with him for lunch. After he learned that it was Sam's favorite restaurant, he understood. It was hard for him, too. If you've ever served on an Army post, you become a big fan of Burger King. They even had one in Afghanistan, at the Bagram Air Force Base.

Troy was a trooper, helping me get through the hardest time of my life and never asking for a thing in return.

Morgan was a lot of help too. Since he worked at home, he continued with his consulting job. Between Morgan's job and the money Dad was making, we didn't need the unlimited checkbook that much.

Morgan and I spent a lot of time with each other over the fall months. Both of us liked to hang out in the library and read. We always had a book going and getting lost in a good story was an excellent way to keep my mind off of Sam. Sometimes I would sit beside him in his office and watch him code. Since my degree was in engineering, it didn't take too long to understand what he was doing. We started talking more and more about it and I was able to write small programs on my own by the time the holidays came around. He was doing a lot of work with creating new apps for the smartphones that were starting to come out on the market. He claimed it was going to be the next big revolution.

Dad made sure all of us kept in shape. He let me mope for precisely one week before showing up at the house at five o'clock one morning in his PT clothes. Mom and Dad were living at their house in town because they wanted the rest of us to have our space. They also wanted a place where we could come and visit when we needed a change of scenery.

The holidays were rough for all of us. It was impossible to get through the season without thinking about Sam all the time. We'd never done much together for Thanksgiving, but Christmas was always special for us. Troy and I fell asleep on the couch for the first time together on Christmas Eve during "A Christmas Story." I woke up in the middle of the night with a raging hard-on because his was pressed against my back. It was the first time I began to feel like it might be okay to take my relationship with him to the obvious next step.

Dane was instrumental in helping me snap out of it and start getting back to normal. We spent most of our time in the shop helping my dad. Troy kept himself busy in the greenhouse as much as possible. Even though it was winter, there were plenty of greenhouses in the area he could buy from. He had a dizzying array of orchids that were going to really be something. We would probably be making some serious money off them in the future. It didn't take too long to discover that Troy was very particular when it came to the conservatory. Mom was the only person he liked having in there with him. He thought Dane and I were too messy.

Two days after Christmas, Dane and I were in the shop. We had been staining garage doors and applying polyurethane to two other sets that would be shipped out in a few days. For the first time in days, we had a little downtime.

Dad was in town on a supply run and a long lunch with Mom, and Morgan was busy making the next zombie shooter game for a developer in Phoenix.

Dane looked at me with a shy smile. "Max, do you think I could get a dog?"

It was the first time I laughed in months. "You don't have to ask my permission to get a dog, Dane. Your name is on the deed too and Jason said you are good with animals."

Dane fidgeted with the rag he was carrying around. "I need something to take care of and train until we get horses in the spring."

It was a necessary wait because we hadn't started on the stables yet, it was too cold to pour concrete anyway. Although I wanted a dog too, I couldn't resist offering a helpful suggestion. There was an undeniable attraction going on between him and my brother and frankly, I didn't know why they were waiting. "If you want something to take care of and train, my little brother is in the study. He could use the help."

Dane snorted in laughter. "I'm telling him you said that."

I stared at him for a moment, "Trust me, it won't shock him in the least."

Dane fidgeted some more. "Are you telling me it's okay to get a dog or that it's okay to spend more time with Morgan?"

"You don't need permission from me for either."

Dane had a look of satisfaction on his face. "Maybe you should get something you can take care of and train too?"

I had a pretty good idea what was going on. "You and Morgan shouldn't worry about me. Troy and I are moving along at our own pace and there's nothing wrong if you and Morgan want to move things along faster than us."

The tears started flowing down Dane's cheeks. It was the first time we had really discussed Sam's death. "He wouldn't want you to be alone, Max." Dane gestured at our surroundings, "I've never felt more comfortable about life and death since I came here with you. Your strength, your family, and our friendship have kept me from falling apart." He took me into his arms and hugged me. "It's okay to be happy, Max. Sam was a great friend, I know he would want the same for you."

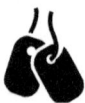

Dane and I were on the way to the local animal shelter within the hour. On the way, he had an idea he wanted to talk about. "I have a business proposition for you."

"Okay, I'd love to hear it."

The words came out of Dane in a rush. "We should get into the initial training of service dogs. There is a huge need for it and it would be an excellent vocation to teach those who are interested."

"How big of a need is there?"

Dane had his facts, "The waiting list for guide dogs in particular, is almost two years."

"You mentioned initial training...We wouldn't be doing the actual service dog training here?"

Dane shook his head. "Service dogs need to learn basic obedience skills before service training. They also have to be old enough for it to be effective, ideally about eighteen months. We would take puppies, maybe two at a time, rotate them through obedience training, and release the best candidates to service dog school." He turned to me with the most earnest look possible. "It would be loads of fun."

"What happens to the dogs that aren't good enough for service dog school?"

Dane's eyes practically sparkled. "Dogs that don't qualify for service training are usually too playful. They would make excellent pets and families would be more than happy to buy a dog that is already potty trained and knows the basics. We could charge a pretty good price for something like that." Then he shrugged, "Or keep a few for ourselves..."

He was being awfully cute, but I still had to ask a few questions. I was going to definitely put the brakes on it if he started talking about getting a bunch of cats. Well, a couple would be all right...Okay, maybe three. "Would we make anything for the dogs that go on to advanced training?"

"We would be paid primarily for their room and board. It's more of a public service than anything." Dane took a breath and gave the best reason of all, "Max, we are very fortunate to be here. This would be a good way for us to give something back. I don't think we should ever lose sight of that."

"I agree completely." I had one more question though, "Do you have experience with this sort of thing?"

Dane nodded. "Max, if you decided to buy an elephant, I could train it. I've always been good with animals. I've worked with all types since I was a little boy."

We didn't have much more time to talk about it because Dane pulled up to the animal shelter.

We made our way through the shelter. Dane found exactly what he was looking for in the second aisle of the dog area, Howard was a handsome two-year-old Border collie mix, Dane stopped in his tracks when he saw him. He had enough excitement for a three-year-old.

"Max, he's perfect. I need a dog that has no problem spending the day outside with me and is good with horses. Border collies are great for that." He smiled and practically ran off, "I'm going to find someone who can help us!"

Howard seemed exceptionally friendly. He started whining when Dane left. I reached my fingers in the chain link and scratched his ears. "Howard, I'm gonna look around, your human will be right back." Howard sat on his haunches and relaxed as if he understood me perfectly. He'd be coming home with us.

I don't know what possessed me to keep on looking. It seemed as if a force I didn't control, was pushing me to go further down the aisle. Since I had plenty of experience with such things, I decided to investigate.

I reached the end. Each of the kennels had a short information sheet about the occupant. There were basics such as the name of the dog, its age and other relevant factors like house training or other skills. The dog at the end had an additional sign on his kennel proclaiming him to be potentially vicious.

He was a big boy too, a full-grown mastiff. He sat on his haunches, calmly watching as I approached. When I stopped and got a good look, his tail began to wag. Didn't seem too vicious to me. I looked at the information sheet, he was one year old. According to the information sheet, his name was Dexter. I liked the name and he seemed like a cool dog.

Dexter stood and pressed his nose to the gate. It was probably stupid, but I stuck my finger in. He gave it a good coating of slobber and practically started dancing in place. Since he liked me, I had to know more about him.

Dane came back with a girl named Tricia. She saw where I was standing and hurried over. "Sir, this dog is not available for adoption. He has been classified as vicious and is scheduled to be euthanized."

I stated the obvious. "Ma'am, this is about the friendliest dog I've ever seen. What makes you think he's dangerous?"

"We use a standard classification developed by the American Humane Society."

Dane stepped forward after he saw I was in love. "What did he do?"

"He snapped at a volunteer when she took his food away."

I couldn't help but laugh. "He's a big dog, he's probably pretty serious when it comes to eating."

Dane interjected again, "We would like to hear his story."

Tricia looked at me and at the dog who was now on his hind legs with his huge paws on the gate. I reached out and squeezed one of them. My hand was instantly drenched with more slobber. "He belonged to a sixteen-year-old boy who was killed in an ATV accident. His family brought the dog in because they couldn't control him anymore. He growled and snapped at anyone who came near him."

Dane had a huge grin when I pulled my hand back, it was practically dripping. I waved it back-and-forth in an attempt to air dry.

Tricia smiled and handed me the hand towel she had sticking out of her back pocket.

I looked back at the dog. He seemed very happy. "Can you let him out with me somewhere? I'd like to see how he acts outside of the cage."

Tricia nodded. "I'd be glad to. I've learned over the years that when a dog is mean to everyone and suddenly turns nice for a certain person, we should investigate." She got a leash off a nearby hook. "We'll take him to one of the observation suites and see how he acts."

Dexter, was a perfect gentleman the entire way. He was obviously well trained, he naturally went to my left side and didn't pull at the leash once.

He also behaved himself when Dane brought Howard in the room with us.

After a very expensive stop at the local pet warehouse store, we were back on our way to the mansion. The bed of the truck was loaded down with two-hundred pounds of dog food, toys, collars, leashes, and doggie beds.

Our property was fully fenced and gated so it wasn't a big deal to let the dogs run free. I knew we made a good choice when they stayed right by us. I was so grateful that I got to spend some quality time with Dane, I knew we were going to be great friends. As we made our way towards the house, I smiled at him. "Thanks, Dane."

He smiled right back. "Don't mention it."

Dexter and Howard were great with everyone. I laughed my ass off when Troy and Dexter chased each other around the yard. I wish I had a camera when Dexter knocked Troy on his ass. Dexter was especially cute around my father, his respect was obvious, he sat beside him and nuzzled his huge head into his leg. It was also funny to see my dad have to adjust his step so he wouldn't get knocked over too.

Mom looked at Dexter and shook her head. "I'm going to bring some beach towels; we'll need them for all the drool."

Everybody cracked up. Dexter got up on his hind legs, with his paws on my shoulders, and licked me in the face. It was the first time I'd felt happy in a long time.

21

January 2007

There was some unfortunate business I had put off too long. It had been pestering me since I got back to Boulder. Dad let me borrow his truck after I explained I needed to go for a ride.

I knew if I wanted to ever be able to move on with Troy, I needed to do something first.

Sam's remains were in a beautiful place with an amazing view of the Flatiron Mountains. I took Dexter with me because I wanted to share the experience with him. I had him on his leash, but it wasn't really necessary. I didn't have to even look that hard, Dexter lead me right to it. I knew how things worked by now, and it brought a lot of comfort to me.

I sat on the sidewalk in front of the granite slab with the dates of Sam's birth and death. It gave me some comfort to see that his parents included his military service under his name. Dexter sat patiently beside me as the sobs took over. He was like a rock, occasionally nuzzling into my face to let me know he was there for me.

I couldn't understand how I would ever be whole again.

Somebody squeezed my shoulder. "I think he'd be happy you came to see him."

I turned to see who was there. It was Sam's father, I stood up to face him. I could barely get the words out, "I'm so sorry he's gone."

"Son, I know how important Sam was to you. It breaks my heart that the two of you won't grow old together."

I had a lot of inside knowledge, I figured it would be okay to share a little without sounding like a religious fanatic. "I know I'll see him again, and so will you."

Mr. Rogers smiled sadly. "Thank you for saying that, Max. That knowledge is helping me and Sam's mother get through all this."

I didn't really know what else to say. Sam's parents and I were never that close. It was one of the biggest drawbacks of our strange supernatural life. The mansion's overwhelming presence never gave Sam's parents much of a chance. "If there's anything I can do for you and Mrs. Rogers, please don't hesitate to ask. Someday I would like to sit down with you and his mom so I can tell you more about him. He was the best friend I ever had. He was a wonderful human being and a kick-ass Army officer. I have a lot of stories that would make you proud."

"Thanks Max, we would love that."

Mr. Rogers put his arm around my shoulder. "Why don't you come to the car with me? I have a few things for you. I spoke to your mother this morning, she told me you would be here."

"Okay."

Mr. Rogers had one of those file boxes people use for important papers. The things he had for me were beyond thoughtful; one of the most important was a picture Morgan took back in our early days, it was black and white, Sam and I had our arms around each other's shoulders. We had our shirts off and were grinning like fools. There was also Sam's favorite CU sweatshirt. More than anything I wanted to bury my face in it to see if it still smelled like him, but I decided that probably wouldn't be the best thing to do in front of his dad. There were a few other priceless artifacts; a paper coaster from the bar where we had our first legal beer, a purple shoelace from the shoes Jason got for him, and the most wonderful of all—his dog tags and his Army ring. I was speechless with gratitude.

Mr. Rogers reached into the box and took out the last two items, both envelopes. "These are for you too."

I recognized the first envelope immediately, my parents had one just like it. When Sam and I got our commissions as second lieutenants, we made a pact to write a letter to each other and our families in the event something happened to us. I was certain that Mom and Dad still had my letters safely tucked away. I wasn't too sure what the second envelope contained.

Mr. Rogers handed the letter to me. "I'm sure you know what this is. You'll probably want to read it by yourself when you get home." He wiped away a tear, "Sam told us what's in here."

I took the letter. "Thank you for giving it to me, this might be the most valuable thing anyone has ever given me."

Mr. Rogers handed me the second envelope. "This is something that Sam also wanted me to give you in the event of his death. Go ahead and open it, he told me it would be okay."

It was a check made out to me for $1 million. I sucked in a breath, "Oh my God!"

"Sam had me take out a life insurance policy before he started his first tour. He told me it wasn't a good idea to have you listed as the beneficiary on his Army life insurance policy because it would've raised a lot of questions. He wanted there to be something for you in case the worst happened. He said you would know how to put it to good use."

I was speechless.

Mr. Rogers gave my shoulder another firm squeeze. "Once things settle down, we'll get together and have dinner or something."

I nodded slowly. "That would be nice, thank you."

Once Mr. Rogers left, I got back in the truck with my faithful dog and started reading.

I was surprised to find that the letter was only a few months old. I'd made a few revisions to my own, but hadn't made any changes for about three years. I couldn't wait to find out what he had to say...

Max...

I think it's important to start off with how much I love you. I have always loved you. Truthfully, I was in love with you before we even met. Back then, I was in love with the idea of you. I loved you during those months we dreamed about each other before we actually met. I loved you the day you opened the door that first time. It took everything I had not to jump you that day, you were so unbelievably hot in your shorts and nothing else.

I know you are sad. It makes me sad writing this because if you are reading it, I'm no longer with you. I realize any attempt I make to make you feel better may make you feel worse. However, we both know how things work and I hope that brings you some relief. I happen to have it on very good authority that my absence will seem like a blink of the eye in the great scheme of things.

Jason and I have talked one-on-one through the years. I've learned a lot from him. Probably the most interesting fact is how you and I are soul-mates. We have been together many times already.

You also have a second soul-mate, as many do. If you have a third or fourth, I don't know, because you know how Jason is with the facts. I'm pretty sure you know who your second soul-mate is. It's time for you to give your attention and your love, to him.

Give Morgan a big hug and a kiss for me. Let him know that I can't wait to see him again, but let him know I expect it to be a long time. The same goes for you as well. You have a special mission you need to see to the end. I'm confident that you will do a good job because you are a good man. I'm confident you already have a plan. I hope the money from the life insurance can help.

Max, I love you and can't wait to see you again. Rest assured, if there is a way for me to see you sooner, I am working on it.

Love, Sam

22

April 2007

It took some time, but we finally got into the swing of things by spring. There were a lot of certification requirements and other hoops to jump through before we could start helping people. Mom and Dad were good at cutting through red tape and getting people to be more helpful when it was required. We would be welcoming our first guest in a matter of days.

Troy and I were still taking things pretty slow. We spent much of our downtime in the library together or talking in the conservatory. More often than not, he spent the night with me, but neither of us were at the point where he started moving his stuff into my room—or mine into his. We weren't to the point where our relationship involved sex.

I knew there was something special between us. We went out on several dates to the movies and some of them involved dinner. More than anything, I was afraid of moving too fast. I could tell he was waiting for me to make the first move.

I finally decided to get my act together in early April. I could see that Morgan and Dane were happy and my heart ached for some happiness of my own. I knew the only way I was going to get it was to ask Troy to be my boyfriend. I was tired of being alone and I had specific knowledge that Troy was the right guy for me. My brain knew it, my dick certainly knew it, and my heart was finally ready to acknowledge it.

I had grand plans for a romantic evening. I went upstairs for a shower, because I figured it would be better to be neat and clean when I asked Troy to spend his life with me. Besides, I'd been outside playing in the dirt all afternoon with Dane and his puppies. We had six of them. The mere sight of those four cute Labrador puppies, and two equally cute German Shepherds was enough to turn my heart to a puddle of goo. Dane was excellent with them.

Dexter loved them too. He patiently tolerated them when they wouldn't leave him alone and he was trying to take a nap.

I was thinking of which movie I'd like to take Troy to as I stepped out of the shower.

I stopped in my tracks when I saw Jason sitting on the bed. He had such a great track record when it came to catching me naked. I voiced my displeasure right away. "You are such an asshole! You didn't even stop by for Christmas!"

Jason took a moment to look me up and down before he said anything.

I stuck my arms out and turned around for him, so he could get a good look.

He grinned. "It's nice to see that your self-esteem is back to normal."

"Bite me, Jason."

Jason crossed his feet at his ankles. "You know my time is limited. If you would like to stand there naked and argue with me, I guess I'll just kick back and listen." He waggled his eyebrows, "And watch..."

"Alright Buchanan, out with it. Why are you here?"

He snapped his fingers and he was suddenly in front of me and he was very naked. There was no denying my automatic response, I *had* to look down.

"Make sure you take a good look," He smirked.

My mouth opened to give him a particularly well thought out reply, but his tongue was in my mouth before I could get the words out.

The kiss lasted for a few seconds. Jason stood back and smiled and looked down at my hard dick. "Well, everything seems to be working!" He snapped his fingers and Troy was standing there instead.

We weren't in the mansion either, it looked like Jason zapped us to the most nondescript hotel room he could find.

It took a minute or two to figure everything out because Troy and I were in the middle of an amazing kiss and we were both naked.

We looked around the room in wonder. Our clothes were neatly folded on the dresser but there wasn't any additional luggage. Apparently we weren't expected to be there very long.

I casually walked over to the nightstand and opened the drawer. There wasn't anything in there, not even a Bible.

Troy laughed. "What are you looking for?"

"Jason is usually pretty good about supplies." I turned towards him and shrugged my shoulders. "Maybe we're not supposed to get to that yet."

Troy smiled and looked down at his hard dick. "There's a lot we could do before it comes to that."

I nodded in agreement as I steered him over to the bed and gave him a little push. I got down on my knees in front of him and smiled. "You are absolutely right."

Troy was on his elbows and he put his foot in the middle of my chest before I could do anything. "You like my big dick, don't you?"

I nodded. His toes weren't that bad either, but I decided his dick would be more fun. I looked up at him. "Is there anything in particular you want me to do with it?"

"Let's see what comes naturally."

I had to give it to Jason, he certainly knew how to get the ball rolling. I leaned in and went down on Troy Atherton for the first time in a few years. It was just as good as I remembered.

After I had a mouthful, Troy returned the favor. He was amazing and got a mouthful too.

Troy got up when we finished and looked out the window. I was more interested in my personal view of his cute butt than what he was looking at. All it took for Troy was one quick look. "That motherfucker!"

"What's wrong?"

Troy pointed angrily out the window. "Jason sent us to my hometown. We're in Colby, Kansas." He took a deep breath, "My dad's landscaping shop is about a quarter mile down the street. I can see it from here."

Jason had such a nice way of interfering, he was getting much more overt the longer he knew us.

I stated the obvious, as I started to pull on my underwear. "I guess it's time to meet your parents, huh?"

Troy stood by the window and sulked.

I helpfully handed his underwear to him. He took them, but didn't put them on.

While I certainly admired the view, I also knew how Jason operated. "Jason sent us here because we agreed to help him with his mission. You have heard all the stories about what homophobia can do." I stated one of the more obvious facts, "I'm pretty sure he didn't send a car for us in the parking lot, so if we want to get back home, we're going to have to do what he wants." I watched Troy carefully to gauge his expression.

Troy put his underwear on, but his expression was still defiant, "Just because I put my underwear on doesn't mean I'm going."

I laughed. "Would you prefer for me to throw you over my shoulder and carry you?"

Troy's cheeks flushed with obvious heat. "In another situation that might be kind of hot."

I smiled and stepped closer. "Duly noted, Captain" Then I flashed a grin, "Now get your ass dressed so we can get this over with."

Troy was so cute as he stomped around the room like a five-year-old. "Fine, dammit!"

I added a further helpful suggestion, "You've been talking about going back here and getting your truck anyway."

Troy pulled on his jeans and walked up to me. He gave me another amazing kiss. "Thanks, Max. I know what you're trying to do."

I acted like I was checking my watch because I wasn't actually wearing one. "In time you will learn its best to go with the flow when Jason gets an idea in his head about something. I'd rather do this voluntarily than have him zap us directly to your father's office."

Atherton Lawn and Landscape was in a metal building on Colby's main drag. The business had an attractive earthen berm with trees and other plantings to show off what they could do. There were two cars and a truck parked in front with the company logo. Off to the side of the building was a fenced area with an open-sided barn for trucks and equipment.

Troy's expression was grim as he reached for the door. "Here goes nothing."

I put my hand on his shoulder before he could open it. "No matter what happens, I have your back."

Troy's smile was sad, weak, and a little lopsided, it was enough to make my stomach churn. "Thanks, babe."

We went inside the building. There was a small reception area with a long counter. There were two ladies on the phone with customers.

Troy continued towards the back and opened the door to an office. He stepped inside, "Hi Dad."

I stayed by his side.

My first impression was Troy must have gotten his smaller stature from his mom because his dad was pretty tall. I sized him up warily because I didn't know what to expect. I felt confident I would prevail if things got physical.

Mr. Atherton jumped to his feet. "What the hell are you doing here?"

"I thought you might like to know how I'm doing, and that I'm okay."

I consciously stepped forward, my hip brushed against his. It was electric.

Mr. Atherton's complexion turned a deep shade of crimson. "It's been made perfectly clear that you aren't welcome here." His gaze wandered over to me. "And I also made it perfectly clear that I don't care to meet any of your faggot friends!"

I stepped forward, "Okay, I think you need to watch your language."

"And you need to shut your mouth!" He roared back.

My reaction was appropriate, I started to laugh, "Is that supposed to intimidate me?" I gestured to Troy. "Your son and I can yell just as loud as you." I smiled, "We've made a career of it."

Mr. Atherton's expression became murderous. He stood up and began to approach me. I held up my hand. "I would strongly advise you to remain where you are. If you want to get physical, I'll put you in the hospital."

"I'm going to throw your asses right out of this building!"

I decided on a different tactic, I pivoted Troy around and lifted the hem of his shirt, pointing at the nasty scar on his lower back. "Do you see this? This is where your son was injured at Fort Bragg. He could have died." My finger traced along his scar and stopped about an inch to the side. "An inch further this way and he would've had only one kidney." I could feel Troy shiver against my touch.

I pulled up the leg of my jeans so he could see some of my scars. "I got this at the same time. If your son hadn't grabbed my arm and started running, I would probably be dead now." I choked up as I thought about Sam. "Your son was an amazing officer in the United States Army. If you want to keep up the name calling, I'll be more than happy to go out the door with him and you'll never see us again."

I stood beside Troy and put my arm around his shoulders. If his dad had a problem with it, too fucking bad. I was going to spend the rest of my life with his son whether he approved or not.

Troy's father visibly deflated. He looked at his son. "Is this true?"

Troy nodded.

"Why didn't you tell me?"

"Because you made it very clear you didn't want to see me again unless I became straight," Troy answered.

I was proud of his no nonsense answer, just like what an Army officer would give.

"Jesus Christ, you could have said something! You could have called us to let us know what you've been through."

Troy was momentarily speechless. I watched as a tear made its way down his cheek, I reached out and wiped it away. I decided to speak since nobody was saying anything. "Mr. Atherton, your son is safe. You obviously have an issue with gay people, so I won't bother you with the details of what we mean to each other, but you can be assured he's safe with me. Troy and I help people, Mr. Atherton. We are in the process of setting up a place where we can help other veterans adjust to civilian life." My arm found its way around his waist. "We have a greenhouse at our place in Colorado and Troy has done a beautiful job." I looked at him proudly and choked up, "We are going to have a wonderful life together."

Mr. Atherton's demeanor changed because he realized the gravity of the situation—he'd almost lost his son. His attitude did a complete one-eighty. "I think that sounds nice." He shook his head. "Troy, I promise to be more understanding in the future."

Troy approached his father and gave him a hug. "That's all I have ever asked."

Mr. Atherton stood back with his hands on Troy's shoulders so that he could observe him and still hold on to him. "I am proud of you and what you have accomplished with your Army career."

I offered him my hand since we had yet to be formally introduced. When Troy's dad took it, I grinned. "I'm Max Carter, by the way."

Troy's dad squeezed my shoulder. "Thank you for being with my son and keeping him safe." He grew concerned, "I'm afraid Troy's mother is not going to be as easy to persuade. Her side of the family has very strong opinions about homosexuality. We are going to have a tough time getting her to come around."

I was touched by the attitude change and his willingness to take on his wife. "Thank you. All we want is a chance to talk. You and your wife deserve to know what a great man Troy is. I sincerely hope we can get to know one another and work through any differences we may have."

The Atherton residence wasn't far from the office. Their house was located on the edge of town, it looked to be on about five acres of land. The house was about twenty-years old and the grounds were spectacular. It was a veritable oasis on the plains. I let out a whistle. "Troy, this is awesome, now I know why you are so good with plants."

When Mrs. Atherton came to the door, I was glad that Troy's dad was with us, she had an impressive scowl. She didn't seem thrilled to see her son or happy to meet me. She was openly hostile as we entered the house, "Typical Troy, always running to your dad first." She pointed an angry finger at her husband. "I suppose they've already worn you down with their rhetoric."

Mr. Atherton sighed, "He's our son. Maybe you should take some time to hear what he has to say."

She looked at her husband. "Homosexuals are an abomination!"

Mr. Atherton shook his head wearily, "Yes, I know how you feel about gay people. I also know how your brothers and your sister feel, too. Instead of rhetoric, maybe we should sit down with our son and his friend so we can get to know them." He took a breath, "These two have been through a lot, and maybe it would do you some good to hear it."

Mrs. Atherton's glare became fixed upon me. "I don't know why *he* needs to be here. We can talk about this among ourselves."

Troy shook his head. "Nope, where I go, he goes." Troy took a seat at the kitchen table and pulled out a chair for me.

Troy's father went to the kitchen to get us something to drink. He came back with four beers and handed them out. "This is probably going to be a beer type of discussion."

Troy's dad was turning out to be pretty cool. Beer wasn't my favorite, but I drank it like it was the best thing to ever pass my lips. That was the way I was brought up.

Mrs. Atherton took a long drink and massaged her temples with her hands. "Homosexuality isn't natural. We can talk all you want, but there's no getting around the central issue."

I joined in the conversation since no one was saying anything. "During my time in the Army, I heard this objection before. I had a friend who grew up on a cattle ranch in Texas. I think he explained it better than I've ever heard before. He told us they would come across a bull from time-to-time who would only mount other bulls. He explained that since homosexuality occurs in nature, it's dishonest to use that argument."

"Nice try," Mrs. Atherton replied. "Animals do not have souls. People do and they can make the choice not to engage in immoral behavior."

"So your objection is religious in nature?" I was more than happy to give my two-cents—I had many years of personal experience to draw from.

"You're damned straight it is." She was very smug with her answer because she had learned about it her entire life.

"I wouldn't be so sure." Jason was so calm with his answer, as if he'd been sitting there the whole time. He looked my way and smiled. "I think I'd better take it from here."

I couldn't resist, giving Jason a hard time was a lot of fun. "I have to admit; I'm starting to enjoy your spontaneity."

Jason's glare was kind of cute. "Smart-ass. I think the two of you need some alone time." He snapped his fingers and we were gone.

23

Troy and I found ourselves standing on the deck of a cabin in the woods. Troy looked out towards the dense forest, the impressive lake, and the mountains. "Do you have any idea where we are?"

I recognized the area instantly, we had vacationed at that very place when Morgan and I were kids. "This is Lake Lure, North Carolina."

Troy looked around. "Are you sure we aren't Upstairs?"

There was an easy way to test where we were, I snapped my fingers for a Coke, nothing happened. "We're definitely in the real world."

Troy stepped much closer. "What are we going to do with ourselves?"

I had several good ideas already, but I had an important question to ask first. "Did you really mean it when you said you'd go where I go?"

Troy nodded solemnly. "How do you feel about that, Captain?"

"Sounds nice…" I took a deep breath. I needed to be sure about something important. "Troy, I'm ready to figure things out between us." I swallowed a couple of times to keep my emotions in check. "I'm probably going to have some guilt with that. I'm not going to get over losing Sam overnight…"

"We don't have to do anything until you're ready, Max." He stepped even closer. "You are worth waiting for."

I pulled him into my arms and kissed him.

Troy was a cutie, he was smart, he liked the same things I did, and he had a lot of amazing talents. I was looking forward to learning from him. It became crystal clear during the confrontation with his parents that I wanted to spend my life with him. Having him in my arms, tasting him, and smelling his clean scent helped cement my decision. I would never forget my first love, but having Troy as the second, wasn't a bad way to go.

I wished I could have figured all this out before Morgan decided to be serious with Dane, but I couldn't be superior to him in everything.

Mom and Dad were lucky; they were going to end up with two more sons. I hoped deep down in my heart that Troy's parents would eventually see it that way.

Troy and I walked inside. The log cabin was a nice place with lots of windows, a leather couch, and two club chairs. There was a large stone fireplace and a small kitchen off to the side and stairs leading up to an open loft. I stood behind Troy with my chin on his shoulder. "Do you want to go upstairs?"

Troy was so cute, he took off on a dead run up the stairs, "Come and get me!"

He was in his underwear by the time I got to him. I gave him a good look and whistled. "Damn, I don't think I'll ever get tired of seeing that."

Troy smiled and took off his underwear. He turned so his firm butt was facing me. I pulled my shirt off and went to him.

Troy turned around. Then I got a good look at his big dick. I waggled my eyebrows at him. "Or that…" Troy sauntered over to me. The boy knew he was about to get some, that's for sure. He hooked his deft fingers in the waistband of my jeans and they were on the floor with my underwear before I knew it. He smiled when he saw me naked.

I kissed him on the nose. "See something you like?"

He answered in the best way possible, he got on his knees and my dick was suddenly deep inside his mouth.

Watching him work his magic was just about more than I could handle, especially the way he looked up at me when his lips reached my pubic bone. He also had a very busy finger, he was tracing that sweet spot behind my balls. He was going to be down there an embarrassingly brief time if he didn't stop pretty soon.

That's when I reached down and pulled him up. I had a feeling he would like it. My hands went from his armpits to his ass in a flash. I picked him up and he wrapped his legs around me. He put his hands on my shoulders and smiled. "I kind of like it when you do stuff like that."

My smirk was automatic, "Duly noted, Captain."

He squirmed in my arms and the lopsided grin returned. "You read me five-by-five, huh?"

I carried him over to the bed and tossed him in the middle of it.

He watched as I crawled up between his legs and took his length in my mouth. He was definitely a mouthful, but I wanted it. Troy was tasty and extra squirmy to boot. It was kind of fun wrestling with him while I gave him a blowjob.

I took my time demonstrating my deep-throating skills in case he had forgotten.

I knew I was in for something different when he hiked his legs up and held them in place with his hands under his knees. I gave his undercarriage a few good licks, because that's what was expected when someone offers up their ass. When I was done, I looked up at him. "I have a feeling I'm not going to be sitting on that big dick of yours this time around."

He reached down and gave me a stroke. Then he became somewhat serious, "I like to keep it fifty-fifty when it comes to bottoming." His brow wrinkled, "I hope that's okay."

I nodded because I didn't want sex with Troy to be like sex with Sam. For the first time in ages, I didn't choke up when I thought of him.

Troy's expression indicated he had the mechanics of it already thoroughly worked out. It caused the temperature in the room to escalate noticeably. "I have something in mind you might like."

Troy had an excellent idea, which I found out after a few hot minutes of preparation. Once I got the condom on, he straddled me facing outward, and took a seat on my cock. His tight heat took my breath away. Once we got going, he placed my hands behind his knees so I could carry all his weight. He certainly got a charge out of being held and carried.

I did too.

Jason got a big charge out of it too, because he decided to drop in right as we got off. He clapped in appreciation. "Nice job, guys!" He walked over to Troy and touched the tip of his finger to his neck. "Here, this will make that hickey go away." He shook his head, "We wouldn't want your parents to see that, now that everything's taken care of!"

Troy and I collapsed in a heap. "Jason, what did you do to Troy's parents?"

Jason made his way to the bathroom and came out after a couple of minutes. He was such a gentleman with the warm washcloth and big fluffy towel. "We had a discussion."

Troy cleaned up and put his underwear back on. He studied Jason with the attention of a seasoned Army officer. "I believe you were asked a direct question. This is not the time to be whimsical."

I was happy that Troy was learning to not take any bullshit from Jason.

Jason took a seat in the chair in the corner and studied his fingernails for an agonizingly long time. "Your mother wasn't getting it, so I had to employ drastic measures."

I stood abruptly, I totally forgot I was naked. I put my hands on my hips and gave him a pointed stare. "Why do you have to talk in riddles all the time?"

Jason looked me over thoroughly and smiled. "I like seeing you in this body."

I was puzzled. "Jason, what are you talking about?"

He shook his head. "I'm sorry, I shouldn't have said that." He looked up towards the ceiling for a moment and nodded. "I've been told in no uncertain terms that I need to get on with it and return to my post." He cleared his throat as he looked at me again. "Um, it would help me concentrate if you put some clothes on."

Troy snickered behind me as he handed me my underwear.

As I sat on the bed, putting on my socks, Jason let us in on a few details. "Troy, I don't think your parents are going to give you any trouble. I took them on a quick tour through the ages so they could see firsthand, what homophobia does to people." He wrinkled his nose, "Even after seeing the dismemberment scene I described on our first Christmas, your mother was still defiant."

Troy was quickly learning how to deal with Jason Buchanan. "And…"

Jason smiled. "Your parents think quite differently now, after meeting Gabe. He always has such a way with words."

Troy looked at Jason in disbelief. "Are you telling me you introduced my parents to Gabriel, the angel?"

Jason nodded. "Yes, but he gets pissed if you refer to him as anything other than Gabe. He tends to embrace modernity more than the others."

Sometimes I thought Jason was full of shit, but there was no way of knowing. "How did that go?"

Jason stood up and handed me my shirt. "Angels are particularly intimidating when they choose to reveal themselves in their natural form. They're not as fluffy as they appear in all the paintings, they also tend to be very loud."

Since Jason and I always gave each other a hard time, there was no reason for me not to do so then. "That's good to know, I thought they went around in trench coats and suits."

Jason laughed. "We all get such a kick out of watching *Supernatural* upstairs. It's a great show." Then he grew serious and stood in front of Troy with his hands on his shoulders. "Troy, your parents are going to be fine and you should have a healthy relationship with them in the future. Just be patient and give them some time."

I reached for Jason's hand. "Thank you, as always."

Jason put his hand over his heart in mock shock. "Holy shit, I think this is the first time you have ever been nice to me!"

Once we were dressed, Jason became serious. "Okay, it's time for the two of you to go back to Colorado and start living." He smiled, "You have a big house, have some kids. No one Upstairs will mind."

He looked up at the ceiling and then to us with a grin, "I probably won't see you for some time. Everything is going according to plan and I have other duties that must be attended to."

Before we could say a word, Jason was gone and Troy and I were standing in my bedroom again.

We were officially ready to get on with our lives.

Epilogue

Independence Day 2007

We had a full house over the holiday. Troy's parents celebrated with us. The change in their attitude was dramatic. They spent almost the entire month of May with us helping to design and build several berms and planting beds on the property.

Dane's parents were also frequent visitors. They had gotten over their issues with gay people years before and wanted to get to know Morgan. They were also taken with the dogs and the horses. They spent two weeks with us in June.

My relationship with Troy was healthy and strong. In a way, we were uniquely suited to be together. The relationship I had with Sam primarily existed around the mansion and the amazing gifts it offered. Troy and I started off in a similar fashion, but our relationship was centered around the Army in the beginning. We were fortunate it gained so much depth because we were together in real time. It was turning into a fun relationship with lots of back-and-forth because that's something we were good at. We would probably call each other *Captain* for the rest of our lives.

We had four former soldiers living with us. Morgan worked with Jake, who had two years of community college under his belt and already knew the basics of programming. Cory and Heath both worked with Dane and the animals. They had the most severe PTSD symptoms, so we kept them away from loud power tools. Mike was our token Marine who mainly needed a place to stay so he could finish college. He and my mom were buddies because he was going to go into counseling. He couldn't have asked for a better mentor.

Dexter, as usual, was right by my side. He was in the lounger to my right while Troy was to my left. It was nice to sit back and relax. I was having a hard time deciding which one of them I wanted in my lap. They were both serious cuddle monsters.

When Dexter jumped out of his lounger and went out to the yard, I decided to follow him because he'd already been to the bathroom. He must have heard or smelled something.

When I got to him, he was whimpering at the door to the shop. I opened the door and followed him in. More than likely, he left one of his toys or a prized bone in the shop and wanted it back. Dogs are famous for that sort of thing.

Suddenly I realized we weren't in the shop, we were in the mansion. We weren't in our mansion either, it was the Upstairs version of the mansion.

I stopped in my tracks when I saw the profile I never expected to see again while alive. Strangely, I wasn't emotional. I felt nothing but happiness when I saw Sam Rogers calmly standing there in his shorts, muscle shirt and flip-flops. "Holy shit!"

He smiled and walked towards me. He snapped his fingers and handed me one of the Cokes that appeared. "You look well."

I grinned. "You look good too, Castiel." It was a good bet Sam had been watching TV with Jason at some point.

Sam snorted in laughter, "Does this mean you're going to be a smart-ass with me too?"

The only thing that kept me from picking him up in my arms and carrying him around was due to the fact he looked nineteen again—and I was in love with Troy.

Sam took a seat on the couch and Dexter climbed up beside him and put his head in his lap. Sam scratched his ears.

"You picked a great day to show up."

Sam became more business-like. Maybe *Jason-like* would be a better way to describe the change. "Max, you know how things work. I've been sent here to discuss an important issue."

"I suppose your time is limited."

Sam laughed, "I wouldn't be from Upstairs if it weren't." Sam picked up one of Dexter's paws. "I bet he weighs at least fifty pounds more than me."

I had a lot of sass built up from not seeing Jason in so long. "Do they have a class up there on how to be opaque?" I shook my head. "You are acting exactly like Jason."

Sam's eyes glittered with amusement and mischief, probably something he learned from Jason too. "Okay, I'll get to it then. You and the others have done a wonderful job. My superiors have decided you are a true warrior and it might be beneficial to have you help us with a few more issues than you originally agreed to."

"Sam, everything has finally settled down and I'm happy for the first time since I lost you. This isn't fair, all of us have given enough already. Morgan is finally relaxed. I'm not leaving him again."

Sam became stern. His expression was dead-serious. He never looked like that when he was alive, even if he was mad as hell at me. "First of all, you will have to be out town for weeks at a time, but all of you are strong and able to deal with it. Second, you are tough. Think about it for a moment, where do you think your strength came from? We have been helping you all along."

I shook my head in disbelief. "You people have been interfering with my life and those I care about for decades. Don't you get it that I'm fucking tired?" I stood up and started to pace.

Sam got up and joined me. He put his hand on my shoulder. "You have worked hard and sacrificed a great deal to remove the stain from the mansion. In fact, you have done so well, it has been officially declared stain-free. Jason has worked his ass off over the decades cleaning up this one part of the world. Our superiors have invested a lot of time and energy with you and the others. They are not prepared to let that investment go to waste."

I crossed my arms defiantly. "Whatever, Sam."

"You are a mouthy fucker sometimes." He huffed in exasperation and looked up at the ceiling. His gaze returned to me. He looked slightly apologetic. "I've been asked to get on with it."

I looked down at the floor. Sam knew I would listen because that's the kind of person I was. That's the way I was raised. Sam taught me a lot over the years, I was a more patient person because of him. I learned how to love someone I wasn't able to see every day. I would cherish the time I had with him forever. Mom and Dad brought me up to follow instructions, to be trustworthy and honest. Morgan taught me how to be a proper smart-ass and Uncle Sam taught me how to be a leader. Troy taught me I could love again after the most profound loss imaginable. In short, I had some pretty good people backing me up. "Fine…"

"We want you to run for Congress."

I looked at him for a moment in total disbelief. "You should probably stay away from the Kool-Aid in the break room, Sam. It's obviously spiked with some good shit."

Sam grinned at me. "The election is sixteen months away so you have plenty of time to mount an effective campaign. You have a distinguished record of service in the Army as an officer. You were wounded during your Special Forces training. Democrats in Boulder's congressional district have a large advantage." His eyes sparkled, "And you are gay. Max, this is a slam dunk."

I started to pace. "What about money? It takes a lot to run a campaign, even if it's a slam dunk."

Sam joined me by the wet bar as I fixed myself a bourbon. He squeezed my shoulder. "You still have the checkbook."

I recognized a superior negotiating position as well as anybody. This would be an excellent time for me to get a few answers. While I was happy to see Sam, I was troubled Jason wasn't there. I hadn't seen him since we were in Kansas. He mentioned something in passing and it had been at the back of my mind since he said it. I swallowed my bourbon and returned to the couch with Dexter. "I'm willing to talk about this if you answer a couple of questions."

Sam sighed and sat beside Dexter and started rubbing his belly when he rolled on his back. "You know I am not allowed to get into specifics. You and I both have plenty of experience with how all this works."

I wasn't going to budge. "You haven't even asked me what I want to know."

Sam summed it up perfectly. It wasn't that big of a stretch that he could read my mind, he did a fantastic job of it when he was alive. "You want an explanation of Jason's absence. While you have a pretty good idea of why he's gone, you would like to know for sure."

I nodded. "In your letter, you mentioned soul-mates. I would like to discuss that as well."

"Max, you already know that Troy is your soul-mate."

"He's not the only one, is he?" It seemed fair to ask. I'd spent my entire adult life working towards a goal that I could discuss with only a few key people. So much was shrouded in mystery. If they wanted me to work for them, then they could at least answer those two questions for me. Hell, I'd run for President of the United States if they would tell me what I wanted to know.

Sam looked pleased with my thought. He looked up at the ceiling and my heart skipped a beat. Sam's gaze returned to me after a painfully long time. He must have been told a lot, Jason had never looked at the ceiling for that long. "Our superiors were not happy with Jason for discussing Gabriel or the nickname that Jason insisted on using. They don't have the progressive sense of humor that Jason does."

I was about to reach out and smack him, so he would get to the point, but I scratched Dexter's belly instead.

Sam reached for my hand. "Max, you and I are soul-mates. You and Troy are soul-mates." He smiled, "Yes, you and Jason were soul-mates as well."

I squeezed his hand. "Anyone else?"

Sam nodded. "You have had several more."

"Is Jason in trouble? I had a feeling we might be more to each other when he said how he liked the body I was currently in."

Sam let go of my hand. "We had to endure a long meeting over that one."

Another question popped in my head. It was something I had been thinking about off and on, "Sam, were Morgan and I ever soul-mates? You know how low his barriers are with me."

Sam looked up at the ceiling again. This time it was for a few seconds and he nodded. "If I answer that question, my superiors want a firm commitment from you."

These were some hard-assed negotiations. "Will I get to deal with you in the future?"

Sam shook his head. "I'm sorry, but seeing you is a one-time deal. I'm here because you have served us so well. They like you Upstairs and they knew you wouldn't deal with anyone else but Jason or myself."

Truthfully, I wasn't that sad. I knew I would see Sam again. "Will I ever see Jason again?"

"Yes, if you agree to run for Congress, he won't be confined to his quarters any longer."

I had so many questions. I took a chance and asked another. "Was he in trouble for kissing me?"

"Yes, we are not supposed to make out with past soul-mates when we are working Upstairs."

I reached for his hand and shook it. "You have a deal, Sam."

Sam shook his fist in the air. "Yes, I did my very first deal!" He leaned over and kissed me on the cheek. Dexter sat up and gave each of us a kiss of his own. Sam grew more serious. "You and Morgan have never been actual soul-mates, but the bond the two of your share is from something that happened in the past."

And that's when I knew. "Oh my God, Morgan and I were the two brothers who were killed by their father on this land?"

Sam didn't have to acknowledge it because the knowledge was already in my head. Instead, he reached in his pocket and handed me two rings. "It's time for me to leave." He arched a brow, "I think you know what to do with these." He leaned in and kissed me on the cheek. A tear fell down his cheek. "Have a wonderful life, Max."

Sam promptly vanished and Dexter and I were in the shop again. I was a man on a mission as I made my way to the patio. I knew what I had to do and I was grateful for the choices I had been given.

I was looking forward to my new happy life and a few extra responsibilities. I didn't mind, I had some great people looking out for me and I had eternity to spend with each of them.

Drew Hamilton likes to write gay fiction about good-looking guys with big hearts. He likes multiple happy endings with a lot of sass. Drew thanks you for your purchase and hopes you had as much fun reading as he did dreaming it up.

Drew appreciates feedback and can be contacted at drew.hamilton.author@gmail.com

You can follow Drew on Facebook: Facebook.com/drewhamilton.author

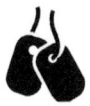

www.ingramcontent.com/pod-product-compliance
Lightning Source LLC
Chambersburg PA
CBHW060153130626
46556CB00006B/2622